D0423705

ANNIE MOORE

THE GOLDEN DOLLAR GIRL

First published in 2000 by Mercier Press
PO Box 5 5 French Church Street Cork

E-mail: books@mercier.ie
16 Hume Street Dublin 2
Tel: (01) 661 5299; Fax: (01) 661 8583
E-mail: books@marino.ie

Trade enquiries to CMD Distribution
55A Spruce Avenue
Stillorgan Industrial Park
Blackrock County Dublin
Tel: (01) 294 2556; Fax: (01) 294 2564
E.mail: cmd@columba.ie

© Eithne Loughrey 2000

ISBN 1 85635 296 X

10 9 8 7 6 5 4 3 2

A CIP record for this title is available
from the British Library

Cover design by SPACE
Cover illustration by Michelle Conway
Printed in Ireland by ColourBooks
Baldoyle Industrial Estate, Dublin 13

This book is sold subject to the
condition that it shall not, by way of
trade or otherwise, be lent, resold,
hired out or otherwise circulated
without the publisher's prior consent
in any form of binding or cover other
than that in which it is published and
without a similar condition including
this condition being imposed on the
subsequent purchaser.

No part of this publication may be
reproduced or transmitted in any
form or by any means, electronic or
mechanical, including photocopying,
recording or any information or
retrieval system, without the prior
permission of the publisher in writing.

ANNIE MOORE

THE GOLDEN DOLLAR GIRL

EITHNE LOUGHREY

MERCIER PRESS

For John

A travelling companion in a million
and without whose help
I'd never have made it to Nebraska.

CONTENTS

1
—

A New Life on Fifth Avenue

Annie awoke with a start. Hearing the clock on the third floor strike six o'clock, she jumped out of bed promptly. She had been dreaming that she was at home in Monroe Street and that Mother was calling her to get up. But of course she was in her own bed in the Van der Leutens' on Fifth Avenue. She'd been working here now for over six months.

She looked around her with a certain amount of pride. She had made this little room very much her own. A narrow bed, a chair and a small chest of drawers were all it had in the way of furniture, but Annie had brightened it up with every little treasure she owned. She had even made a little pair of white muslin curtains to decorate the small attic window which looked out across Central Park. Now that it was spring, the tops of the trees looked as green as any field you'd see in Ireland.

Goodness! she thought. She should have been downstairs by now. Cook would have her guts for garters if she was late again. Luckily, she'd laid the covers in the breakfast room the night before, so at least she had a head start.

She washed quickly in the cold water she'd carried up the night before, scrambled into her black dress, grabbed a newly laundered white apron, and after brushing it out, she swept her hair up hurriedly under her cap and ran down the stairs as quickly and quietly as she could.

She had been warned not to thunder past the second floor where the family slept. Pausing on the first floor she took time to glance into the breakfast room to make sure all was in order. The fire wasn't lit yet. She hoped Peggy hadn't been late or there would really be murder. Peggy, the scullery maid, was obliged to get downstairs by half-past five in order to get the kitchen stove lit and well warmed before Cook started breakfast. But to Annie's relief, all was in order. Peggy not only had the stove lighting but was on her way up to the breakfast room with a bucketful of coal when Annie came into the kitchen.

Poor Peggy. Annie pitied the girl, who was only fifteen and had already been two years working as a scullery maid. The dirtiest of all jobs fell to Peggy and she worked longer hours than anyone else in the household as far as Annie could see. She was always in trouble, but, while Annie felt sorry for her, she knew Peggy brought it on herself. She was the clumsiest girl she'd ever met and Annie felt it was because she never listened to what anyone was telling her. She was always daydreaming and then she'd try to make up for lost time by doing things in a hurry and getting all mixed up. She had been given her notice twice – once when she'd nearly set the drawing-room curtains alight by running to the window with a red-hot poker in her hand. She had been tending the fire when she'd heard the doorbell ring and had run to the window to see who was outside. On another occasion – before Annie's time – she'd dropped a tray full of the Mistress's best china and broken it all. But each time, she broke down in such a storm of tears about how her mother would kill her and how her family needed the money that the Mistress had relented and let her stay on as kitchen-maid. She was now on her last warning though, Annie heard the Mistress tell Cook.

'Good morning, Mrs Parsons, Ma'am,' said Annie in her politest tone to Cook, who was clattering about with pots and pans before cooking breakfast. Cook just sniffed and darted her a black look. You had to keep on the right side of Cook, especially in the mornings.

'How about our breakfast, girl? I told you to have the covers laid here before you retired for the night.'

Annie had only remembered this morning and had hoped to beat Cook to the kitchen and have the table ready by the time she got up. 'Beg pardon, Mrs Parsons.' You had to apologise to Cook always or it would be the worse for you later. 'I'll not forget again.'

She hurried to the dresser and started to prepare the table for the staff in the large, basement kitchen. It wasn't as if it was a leisurely meal. Heaven knows, you'd barely time to eat a bite before it was time to start carrying the heavy trays upstairs for the family's breakfast. Annie would carry up the cold foods first – sliced meats, cheeses, breads – and then she would bring up the cooked dishes and place them under the chafing dishes to keep warm. Breakfast was the one meal Annie served on her own. Arthur, the Van der Leutens' butler, would be in attendance at lunch and dinner.

Mr Van der Leuten, a tall, grey-haired, well-groomed man, a little stooped, was usually the first to come to breakfast. He liked to breakfast alone while reading the newspapers. He left the house early and was at business all day. If the family dined at home, he usually retired to the library the moment the meal was over. Sometimes he even did this if they had company. He seemed kind, Annie thought, but was so absent-minded and quiet in his ways that Annie wondered if he was aware of her presence at all. He lived in a world of his own and she had rarely even heard him speak. When he did, it was to his sons and it was always about business. When his wife was present, he just nodded and seemed happy to agree with everything she said.

The Mistress was a strange one. Occasionally she would smile at you if she met you on the staircase, Annie noticed, but mostly she just swept by as if you were a speck of dirt. 'Twas said she'd fire you if you looked crooked at her. It depended on the nature of the offence, according to Gertrude, the chambermaid.

'How does Peggy get away with so much?' Annie asked Gertrude once.

'The Mistress pities Peggy, you can see that,' replied Gertrude. 'What angers the Mistress most is if the staff get too big for their boots or insolent.' Annie had good reason before long to remember that conversation.

The sons of the family were a lively pair. They were

like grown-up versions of her own brothers Anthony and Philip, Annie thought. You always knew when they were home, they made that much noise, especially Robert, the younger one. He was seventeen and a cadet at West Point. He only came home on holidays but invariably brought friends to stay and it would seem to Annie that the house was full, there was that much to do. Charles was in business with his father but was not at all like him in any way. He resembled his mother in looks and in lifestyle, leading a busy social life and dining out most of the time.

Annie still marvelled at the lives the Van der Leutens led. She had never seen anything like it. Even after two years in America, it was a shock to see how a wealthy family lived. She had not known such style existed. Situated on the fashionable end of Fifth Avenue near Central Park, the Van der Leutens lived in a large, imposing, brownstone house with steps up to the front door, which was used only by the family and company. There was a basement entrance used by Annie and the rest of the staff and a back entrance leading to the stables and coach house.

It was all a far cry from 32 Monroe Street in the Lower East Side, where Annie had started out in America and where her family still lived. Annie had been thrilled to start work for the Van der Leutens, and had been especially excited by the prospect of moving to a house where she would have a room of her own and good food to eat and fine surroundings from where she could see the gentry come and go. But she had underestimated how much she would miss family life

– especially now that the family circle had been enlarged to include her beloved Auntie Norah and Uncle Charlie, who had come to America the year before to join them and indeed were not living far from her parents. Still, she managed to get home to see them all most Sunday afternoons. She had Thursday evenings off too but counted on those to get to a night class or to see her friends. She only occasionally got to see her first friend in America, Sophia Rostov, who would shortly qualify as a nurse at Bellevue Hospital but she saw quite a bit of Molly, who was training to be a kindergarten schoolteacher and was now walking out with Annie's older brother, Tom. Annie suppressed a sigh of envy at the lives both these friends lived. They seemed so free compared to her.

However, for the umpteenth time she reminded herself how well off she was. Three dollars a week with full board and lodging and little opportunity to spend money meant she could now save quite a lot each week. Besides, it was a whole lot better than three dollars a week being slave-driven at the Phoenix Laundry. The mere thought of the laundry and all that had happened there – the long hours, the back-breaking work and finally, the fire which had claimed eleven lives – never failed to cure Annie's feelings of loneliness and she soon realised how lucky she was even to be alive.

'Annie, Annie, come quickly and braid my hair – you promised.'

Annie's heart lightened at the sound of Amy, the Van der Leutens' youngest child, petulantly calling her from the top of the back stairs as she returned to the kitchen.

'Such a tarradiddle,' snorted Cook. 'That child ought to be able to braid her own hair at ten years of age. You have her rightly spoilt.'

Annie knew that Amy could braid her own hair but she was so hurried going out to Miss Merrington's Academy of a morning that she would look like a haystack if she didn't have someone to help her. She also knew that Amy loved to have Annie fuss over her as her Mama was much too preoccupied to have time for that kind of nonsense.

'Go on up, you, and eat your breakfast and I'll be with you by and by. You know I'm busy,' called Annie, smiling at the sight of young Amy, with her pinafore askew, her shoes unbuckled and her hair all over her face. Annie, who had no sisters, greatly enjoyed the Van der Leutens' youngest child, which was just as well, as she had been given special responsibility for her and had to see to her when she came in from school and escort her wherever she went.

Although Amy had been quite indulged and Annie marvelled at the privileged life she led, she could see that, for all that, Amy was quite a lonely child. Although often cosseted, Annie couldn't help getting the impression that she was something of an encumbrance to the family, especially to her mother, whose hectic social life seemed to take precedence over everything else. Amy's existence seem to go almost unnoticed by her parents apart from the occasional pat on the head from her father and the rather formal greetings and leave-takings which seemed to be a large part of the communication between mother and daughter. Certainly, she was indulged by her brothers but they weren't often around. Amy adored Robert and lived for the holidays, when he was more often at home. But in the meantime, Annie was the one who really looked after her.

Annie looked upon Amy as a godsend who helped to fill the loneliness she often experienced since she'd come to work here. To come from the heart of a loving family who lived as close as peas in a pod to the splendid and spacious house on Fifth Avenue was an experience that had made Annie really value her family life. She missed the rough and tumble of her two younger brothers and the easily shown affection of her parents and noticed that her employers, of upright Dutch stock, were not prone to displays of affection of any kind.

As soon as breakfast was over and Amy had left for Miss Merrington's, Annie settled down determinedly to her chores. Thursday was one of her toughest days. There were extra weekly tasks to be done on a Thursday and they had to be completed before she could escape for her one evening out in the week. But she was in luck today.

'Annie, the Mistress says we don't need to clean the windows today as someone is coming to work on the front of the house and they would soon be soiled again. She says to do it next week.' Gertrude looked as pleased as punch about this. But then Gertrude always looked pleased. Annie liked her. She was about twenty-five, quite plump, with flaxen hair braided tightly around her head. Of Swedish family, she had come from Nebraska two years previously to find work in New York. But Gertrude was a country girl at heart and told Annie that when she had saved just a little more money, she intended returning to Nebraska for good. She had a sweetheart there, she confided, and they would be married on her return.

Gertrude reminded Annie of Ellen King, her Irish friend whom she'd met on the ship on the way to America and with whom she still corresponded. Ellen had been bound for Nebraska and was now married to an Irishman she'd met there and was expecting her first child.

In the dining room, Annie settled down to cleaning the silver, which had to be polished in readiness for Mrs Van der Leuten's At Home on the following evening. Down in the kitchen the atmosphere was already becoming heated in every sense of the word as Cook prepared some of the food in advance. She and Gertrude exchanged grimaces outside the kitchen door as they heard Cook shouting angrily at poor Peggy who, as usual, couldn't do anything right.

'Clean is it? Clean indeed! I'll give you clean, you stupid girl! There, wash those plates again I tell you. They'll not do for the Mistress's guests.'

Peggy was in tears and no wonder, thought Annie, stuck as she was in the kitchen all day struggling to meet Cook's high standards. The poor girl wouldn't even be taken with the family and the rest of the staff to Newport in Rhode Island, where the Van der Leutens had a summer home and where they would be moving in a few weeks' time to spend the summer months. Peggy would be left, at the mercy of Cook, along with the coachman and the gardener to look after the upkeep of the town house.

'Please God I get away in time for I've to meet Molly after my class this evening,' Annie confided to Gertrude as they carried the Turkish rugs out to the garden together to brush and air them.

'Don't fret, Annie. I will be here if the Mistress is looking for something to be done this evening,' soothed Gertrude, who seldom went out and liked nothing better than to sew samplers in her little room of an evening. 'For my trousseau,' she'd told Annie once.

'Thank you, Gertrude,' Annie replied, knowing, however, that if the Mistress got it into her head to give Annie work to do this evening, she would do so and that would be that. It had happened before, making Annie feel more like a prisoner than ever. She could never depend on having her time off. It was at the Mistress's whim and she had had to get used to that.

Meeting Molly was Annie's lifeline to the real world and tonight Molly had something special to discuss with her. Annie was dying to know what it was about. Molly also kept Annie informed about Mike Tierney, whom Annie saw little of these days. Molly, like Annie's older brother Tom, was active in politics and often went to meetings and talks at Tammany Hall, where Mike spent most of his free time. Mike was a tailor by profession but his main passion was politics. Annie had first met him on her voyage from Ireland to America two years ago. He had since become a very special friend to her and to the family. He had been a great support to Annie when the laundry had closed down. He had managed to get her some piecework from his business to keep her going before she had been hired by the Van der Leutens.

travel, she thought, and see the world in style or be someone famous who was admired and written about in the journals and newspapers.

2

PLAYING TRUANT

Molly was waiting at the entrance to the night school where Annie took a weekly stenography and typewriting class. It had been Molly's idea to encourage her friend to acquire a skill that would give her possibilities to get out of domestic service at a later stage. Molly – who was now nineteen and coming to the end of her second year at teacher-training college – knew that Annie was very smart and would not want to stay in service for very long. She had not had much choice, of course. After the fire had destroyed the laundry the only other job Annie could have found would have been as an ill-paid factory worker. Molly knew that Annie's only way to some kind of independence at that point was to take the opportunity to go into service, where she would be able to save some money.

Molly, from an Irish background herself, was sympathetic to the plight of Annie's family, who, like most immigrants, had a hard struggle to get on in the United States. But now at long last, they were beginning to succeed. Matt Moore, Annie's father, had been promoted again in the past year, which was just as well as his wife Mary Moore now had little Patrick to look after as well as the two older boys Anthony and Philip, and she found little enough time to take in the sewing work that the family had partly depended on a few years back.

Tom, Annie's older brother, was doing well too. Having started as a bellhop in the Excelsior Hotel, he had now worked his way up to the position of head porter. His main interest in life now, however, was politics and like Molly he belonged to the local branch of the Democrats. He had confided to Molly that he would like one day to run for election.

Molly could see that staying on in service indefinitely was not the right thing for Annie. Already after six months, she could see her friend becoming restless. No wonder: she worked day and night in the same environment and although she had Sunday afternoons and Thursday evenings off, she was at the beck and call of her mistress and these free periods could be cancelled at a moment's notice should they not suit the household. Already, she had missed two of her classes but Annie was an eager student and soon made up the lost time. All the more reason for Annie to have sensible plans for the future. She would make an excellent office clerk, Molly thought, if she could finish her course and qualify.

Annie appeared, breathless, at the foot of the staircase. 'I'm truly sorry to be so late, Molly, but Miss Myers didn't hear the bell and she just continued right on.'

'Annie, it's no matter. Let's go and have some tea.' As soon as they reached the tea-rooms Annie sank into her seat gratefully. She'd been on her feet and working hard since six o'clock that morning.

'I have much to tell you,' Molly began. 'You know I have joined the City Women's Suffrage League, Annie?'

'Is that to get us women the vote?' Annie asked, wide-eyed. 'It could never be, Molly. Father says no one would stand for it. He says . . . '

'Don't be minding him, Annie. And don't let Tom hear you saying such a thing. He's a supporter. You should join us too, Annie. The League is organising a big petition to get women to be included on the ballot. Women everywhere are signing it. And today I went to a meeting and they announced that all working women should have a chance to sign it.'

'Not me, Molly. I could never arrange it. It's as much as I can manage to get to my class and to see the family on Sundays. I wouldn't dare ask.'

'No, Annie, you don't understand. They need people just like you to sign and you could do it some evening on the way to night school. I will find the nearest place for you. They will stay open late especially for working girls.'

Molly could be very persuasive and reminded Annie how interested she'd been in getting better conditions for women when she worked in the laundry.

'Besides, 'twas Mike Tierney who told me he thought you might be interested in it,' she added slyly. Molly wasn't blind and it hadn't escaped her notice that whenever Mike was around or even mentioned, Annie perked up. 'You see it's not only to get women the vote, Annie,' she went on to explain. 'The League is working towards equality for women in every way, especially to get better working conditions and unions and things like that. Here, look at this.' She handed Annie a sheet of paper outlining what the League's goals were. It explained that the vote for women and membership of trade unions for women were its two main aims. Annie's face brightened. Molly knew that would make an impact. Annie had spent a lot of energy trying to get the women in the Phoenix Laundry interested in a trade union before the fire. Remembering now how incensed she had felt about working conditions in the laundry, Annie knew her friend was right. It didn't seem right now that she was in a new job and being well paid that she should abandon what she had felt so passionately about only a year before. Yet she couldn't help but worry about what the Mistress would say if she were to find out.

As if reading her thoughts, Molly persisted. 'No one need know, Annie. It's your own business entirely. It doesn't mean you're rebelling or going on strike or the like,' she laughed.

'You're right, Molly. I may be someone's servant but they don't own my mind now do they? I'll join the League too if you'll help me to find a place nearby to sign the petition.'

Molly clapped her hands, delighted. 'I knew you'd join us,' she cried.

*

Annie was as good as her word. She slipped out of the house early one evening, a few days later, without a word to anyone. It wasn't her time off and the Mistress would surely have refused had she asked permission. She threw a shawl over her work dress and dashed to the corner of Seventy-sixth Street, where she had arranged to meet Molly. Her friend, usually prompt, was about twenty minutes late, leaving Annie to pace anxiously up and down the sidewalk hoping not to be spotted by anyone she knew. Finally, Molly arrived out of breath.

'Sorry, Annie, I really could not help myself. The trolley-car got stuck halfway down Seventh Avenue and I had to leave it and walk the rest of the way,' she explained, taking Annie by the arm and leading her up town towards Pacific Hall on East Broadway, where, she told Annie, she could sign the petition and become a member of the City Women's Suffrage League all at the same time.

Annie couldn't help but be excited when she saw the crowds of women gathered to sign the petition. There was a separate group of women on a platform at the top of the room – one was called Miss Adele Field and it was she, Molly pointed out, who would speak shortly and explain to the women what it was all about.

'But, Molly, I am not supposed to be out at all,' Annie told her friend. 'Can I not just sign the paper and leave? I thought it would just take a few minutes to do this. I must not wait for the speeches.'

'But that's the best part,' said Molly, her face falling. 'I so much want for you to hear what it's all about. More and more women are hearing about it and joining in the work. I promise you will not regret it.'

Annie agreed reluctantly and before long Miss Field

opened the meeting and spoke to the women gathered there.

'I welcome you here this evening, ladies, and want you to know that you are greatly helping the cause of women's suffrage by taking this step. The amendment to be introduced during the coming Constitutional Convention will provide for the striking out of the word "male" from the qualification for voters.'

She continued for another ten minutes and Annie shifted restlessly in her seat, unable to fully understand or concentrate on what this fine lady was saying for worrying about the time. By the time she came to sign the petition all she wanted was to escape and be on her way. As soon as she had signed it, she said goodbye to Molly and flew as fast as her legs would carry her up Fifth Avenue. It was a whole two hours since she had left the house. Oh pray God the Mistress had not found her missing.

As she drew nearer the house she saw James, the coachman, drive the brougham down the lane and into the coach house. She ran quickly through the gate behind the coach, trying to keep out of his sight. Then, slipping through the kitchen garden, she made quickly for the back door, hoping no one was watching her from an upstairs window. She tried the door – it was locked. Oh no, surely Cook hadn't retired for the night already, but it seemed she had, as had the others. The kitchen and scullery were in darkness.

What was she to do? Surely she wouldn't have to go up to the front door and pull the doorbell? The Mistress would kill her. Then, suddenly, she remembered the pantry window. It was nearly always left slightly ajar at the top to keep the food as cool as possible in warm weather. Not wasting another second, she climbed up on to the window sill and felt for the gap at the top with her hand. Yes, thankfully, it was open. Quietly and carefully, she pulled the sash down as far as it would go. Luckily, it was a low enough window but only just large enough for Annie to squeeze through. Thank God, she had made it, she sighed with relief. She would never take that chance again. She tiptoed out of the pantry, through the kitchen and up the back stairs. As she opened the door into the vestibule, the clock struck ten o'clock. My goodness, she hadn't thought it was that late. And suddenly, to her horror, just as she made to ascend the staircase, there was Mrs Van der Leuten, standing watching her at the foot of the stairs.

'Follow me,' she directed, opening the door of the library. Annie, her heart beating hard, followed her in and shut the door behind her.

'Where have you been, may I ask?' The Mistress's tone was ice-cold. 'And what do you mean by leaving the house without a word to anyone?'

'I beg your pardon, Ma'am, I did not mean . . . that is . . . I only went to see a friend, Ma'am, for a short while . . . but it took longer than I intended,' Annie stammered, her voice fading as she looked once more at the Mistress's expression.

'Which friend? Was it a gentleman friend?'

'Oh no, Ma'am. It was Molly. She's a real good friend. She . . . ' The Mistress cut her short.

'How dare you, girl, you impertinent girl. How dare

you leave your post without permission. I've been watching you and you're a mite too big for your boots.' The Mistress had raised her voice considerably and Annie feared the whole household would hear her.

'This is a respectable household and you would do well to see that you follow the rules here. If you do not you will soon find yourself out searching for another position and without a character.'

'I am so sorry, Ma'am. I should never have gone. I am truly sorry, Ma'am. Please give me a chance,' Annie implored, convinced that the Mistress was about to sack her right then and there.

'I will brook no further disobedience, I assure you. Sister Bonaventure assured me you were from a good family.'

'Oh I am Ma'am, I am.' Annie was close to tears, wishing her mother were there now to defend her.

'You will go to bed now and you may not leave the house again for a full week, except for the discharging of your duties. Is that quite clear? I will be watching you closely and if there is a recurrence of this kind of behaviour, you would do well to start looking elsewhere. Be off now.'

Anne needed no second bidding. She hastened upstairs to her little room at the top of the house. Looking out at the stars from her tiny attic window, she suddenly felt as lonesome as if her family were at the other side of the Atlantic. She knew she had been in the wrong but to listen to the Mistress you'd think it was a crime she had committed. Tears of frustration filled her eyes. She promised herself there and then that she would indeed look elsewhere. But she would bide her time, save as much money as she could and whatever work she found to do in life, she vowed to herself that she would not work as a servant again.

3

OFF TO THE SEASIDE

The house on Fifth Avenue was buzzing with activity. The Van der Leutens' annual exodus to Newport was in full swing and Annie was working so hard that she missed all her time off for a whole week. Apart from the house having to be cleaned from top to toe, all the furniture had to be draped with large dust covers that were kept especially for the purpose.

'You'd think it was Ireland we were off to for all the preparations we have to make,' Annie told her mother and Auntie Norah one Sunday evening late in May, her last visit before her departure to Newport.

''Tis well for you, Annie, off to the seaside while we bake here in the heat all summer long,' sighed Mother as she planted baby Patrick on Annie's lap and started to prepare supper for the family. Annie loved nursing little Pat, as he was called, though indeed he was not little any more. She dandled him now on her knees, playing 'Pattacake', while he squealed with delight.

Auntie Norah, watching her niece, marvelled at how she had grown up since she had come to live in America two years ago. The girl of just fifteen she'd waved off at Queenstown had matured into a young woman. 'Twas hard to credit. Would Annie have changed so much had she stayed in Cork, she wondered, or was it all the different experiences she'd had in this new world that had changed her?

'Perhaps you'll all get out to Coney Island and go bathing when the hot weather comes,' suggested Annie. 'Remember the fun we had there last summer?'

'Yes, but you'll be living right next to the ocean and you will be able to dip in it nearly every day. And you'll be meeting all the quality too, Annie. You must write often and tell us about it at least,' said Auntie Norah enviously.

'Meet them, is it?' said Annie scornfully. 'Curtseying to them and taking their hats and cloaks and showing them into the drawing-room, but 'tisn't meeting them I am. They don't even look me in the eye. It's "Annie, fetch this" and "Annie, do that", though they don't even know me and never a please nor a thank you.'

'Shush, now. 'Tis very uppity you're getting young lady. You're mighty lucky to have that fine job and to be earning such a good wage.' Mother had begun to worry about Annie's attitude to her elders and betters since she had left home and gone to work for the Van der Leutens. Goodness knows, she didn't realise just how fortunate she was to have got the job in the first place. If it wasn't for Sister Bonaventure at the convent, she'd never have been so well placed. She said as much now.

'Stop worrying, Mother, but 'tis true what I say and

if you were there you'd see how it is. Never fear, I won't let Sister Bonaventure down. But I'm saving my money against the day I'll leave there and get a better job.'

'Better not let your father hear you talking like that,' Mother warned.

Auntie Norah tried not to smile at this exchange. She couldn't help having a certain sympathy with her niece. She knew that being a servant was not easy, for all that Annie appeared to her family to be having a great life.

Annie fell silent. Her mother had hit on a sore point. The last thing she wanted was to cross swords with her father. They had had their differences on occasion since Annie had come out to America and she knew that any kind of independent talk from her was something he just wouldn't countenance. He had snorted with derision one Sunday when she had told him about the suffragists' petition shortly after Molly had told her about it. Lucky she hadn't told him she'd signed it herself.

'Mad as March hares, those silly women. Where do they get these notions? They haven't enough to keep them busy, I'll be bound.'

Cross words were soon forgotten however, as the family arrived home, all thrilled to see Annie, who hadn't made an appearance for the past few weeks. They all crowded around the table in the cramped kitchen and Annie couldn't help but notice that her family's main living room was scarcely the size of one of the Van der Leutens' bathrooms.

Father, Uncle Charlie, Anthony and Philip had all been fishing on the docks and were in fine form, Uncle

Charlie teasing them all and calling Annie 'Copperknob' as he used to do in the old days. That was the great thing about Auntie Norah and Uncle Charlie being with them in America. They made everyone feel more light-hearted and reminded them so much of the more easygoing life they had left behind in Ireland. Though indeed there wasn't anything easygoing about the couple's new life in Amer-ica. Charlie worked all the hours that God gave down in the Fulton Fish Market. He said he felt at home there because it reminded him of the Butter Market in Shandon. Auntie Norah, mean-while, had found a position assisting in a downtown store.

Over supper, Annie told them all about Amy, who was someone they never tired of hearing about. To the boys it was like hearing a fairy tale. She seemed to them like a little princess, such a charmed life she lead.

'And does she really go to school in a carriage?' Philip asked for the umpteenth time, sure it just couldn't be true.

'I'll wager she's right spoiled,' Anthony said, curling his lip disdainfully.

'That's what Mrs Parsons thinks too,' said Annie. 'But she's a little darling and real lonesome. She has not a soul to play with. Some day I'll see if I can bring her to visit.'

This gave the boys something to think about – prin-cesses were fine to hear about but meeting one in real life might be a bit too much of a challenge. But one Sunday shortly prior to her departure for Newport, Annie arrived at 32 Monroe Street accompanied by

Amy. The Mistress had not been at all agreeable to the idea but Amy had begged so persistently to be allowed go that she had eventually been persuaded.

James had brought them some of the way in the brougham as Amy could hardly be expected to walk such a long way but Annie got him to drop them at the corner of Orchard Street because she did not wish to be seen arriving in such a grand vehicle. However, he arranged to call right to the door to collect them later on. The Mistress's orders, he said. They had hardly taken two steps, however, when they were greeted by Philip running eagerly towards them. He had been watching out for them for hours, he said, and thought they would never come. Amy and Philip hit it off immediately, Philip telling Amy all about his visit to the menagerie in Central Park with Uncle Charlie.

'Betcha never saw the alligators,' he said. 'But best of all were the elephants. They're called Juno and Little Tom.'

'Sure I saw the alligators,' countered Amy. 'And the elephants too. And I saw Tip, the wicked elephant, before they killed him. He was too strong to die and they had to put poison in his food.'

Philip looked at Amy with growing respect. Not even Anthony had seen the famous Tip before they had had to put him down last May.

When they arrived, Annie could see that Amy was somewhat taken aback at the poky little apartment which was her family's home. But she greatly admired the little girl for her ability to conceal her feelings and greet Mother and Father and the others as if she were in her mother's plush drawing-room. The family were enchanted with her and they were soon all having a fine time, with Uncle Charlie performing the pick of his magic tricks in order to entertain her. After they had eaten some of Mother's apple pie they settled down to a sing-song and Uncle Charlie treated them all to his rendering of 'Oh Susannah', accompanying himself on his banjo, which delighted Amy.

All too soon James arrived to collect them and Amy had to bid a reluctant farewell to the family.

'Farewell, Princess,' said Uncle Charlie, bowing to her impressively. From that moment Amy was christened 'Princess' by the Moores and would always be referred to thus.

'What fun it was, Annie,' she sighed, sitting back in the carriage, wreathed in smiles. Annie was delighted to see her young charge so contented and she knew that Amy would treasure the memory of the visit, as would Annie herself.

*

The next day Annie learned that she and Gertrude would be departing for Newport by train the following Friday. They could then ensure that everything was in order for the family, who would follow on the Sunday. Mr Van der Leuten and Charles would stay in New York because of their work and visit on weekends. Annie anticipated another frantic week of preparations and hoped she would get an hour or so to say goodbye to Molly.

Next day being Monday, the laundress Lizzie Fother-
gill was installed in the kitchen from early morning, and
by the time Annie came down Lizzie had started in on
the weekly wash. This required copious amounts of hot
water, which had to be heated on the stove and then
poured into the heavy cast-iron tubs. From her days in
the Phoenix Laundry Annie knew just how much work
that entailed.

The following day Lizzie would be back again and
the heavy flat irons would have to be heated on the
stove. Then Annie, Gertrude and Peggy would all have
to pitch in and help Lizzie iron the mounds of laundry.
And there certainly were mounds, especially this week,
with all the clothes to be prepared for the holiday
months at the seaside.

Despite this, however, Annie enjoyed wash days.
Lizzie was the greatest of fun and regaled them with
tales of her doings as they worked. Even Cook brightened up on the days Lizzie was in the house. There was
a hint of festivity in the air and Cook had less to do,
as only cold food could be served because the stove was
in use all day for heating water and flat irons. Annie
loved hearing Lizzie talk about the other houses she
worked in. She had a colourful way of relaying gossipy
tidbits about what went on in the homes of her other
ladies.

They learned that the Denver Blakes had sailed for
the Old World to spend the summer – Annie now
understood this meant they had gone to Europe.

Lizzie then went on breathlessly to describe the
splendour of a great society wedding. 'I heard all about

it at the Abercrombies' last week. The Mistress there was at it and 'twas said that the bride was the most beautiful ever and had a lace train to her wedding gown that was nearly a mile long. She married a count – ain't that somethin'? But for all he's a count he could be a bad egg after all, for he had his bachelor party at the Waldorf and they say the frolickin' went on till morning.' Her brow darkened in disapproval.

The week passed quickly after that and Annie managed after all to get out to meet Molly for a short time on Thursday evening. She found her friend in high fettle, full of plans for the summer months. She was also able to bring Annie up to date on what the City Women's Suffrage League had been doing.

'Aren't you glad you signed the petition, Annie,' Molly asked. 'We now have nearly 182,000 names to it and the list is getting longer every day. Some day soon, for sure, you and I will be able to vote – just like the men.'

'Father will never believe it, Molly. Are you sure 'twill happen. What does Tom say?'

'Well, he can tell you himself, for here he comes,' laughed Molly, as Tom made his way through the crowd towards them, removing his hat and bowing to them in a ridiculous way that made Annie laugh too. Then she saw that he was followed by none other than Mike, and her face lit up. She had not seen him in a long time. Her joy was short-lived though as she saw that accompanying Mike was a tall handsome girl with a banner of dark hair and a bold stride. She suddenly wished that she was not wearing her dowdy working clothes.

'I didn't know Clara was coming too,' Molly said in a low aside to Annie, having taken in her friend's reaction at a glance. Annie's face had clouded over but she soon recovered and stood up welcomingly to greet Mike and the young woman.

Clara Stevenson, Annie was to find out, was one of Mike's political friends from Tammany Hall.

'I've heard about you,' she told Annie immediately. 'You're Tom's sister and you work as a servant girl.'

Annie found her forthright manner a little alarming but Clara smiled charmingly as she spoke, which helped to soften what she said.

'She's much more than that,' intervened Mike, smiling across at Annie. 'You haven't heard all about our Annie. She's famous you know.' To Annie's great embarrassment he proceeded to relate how he had first met Annie boarding the steamer at Queenstown and of her subsequent arrival in America. Then he went on to tell the story of the fire in the Phoenix Laundry and how Annie had barely escaped with her life. She could have killed him.

Clara listened with great interest, looking at Annie with new eyes.

'And she's signed the petition,' added Molly proudly.

'Yes,' said Clara, 'I can see why Annie would have a special interest in the petition.' Annie was unsure quite what Clara meant by that but decided it must be something positive as when she looked up Clara was smiling across the table at her. Yet something in the encounter made her uncomfortable. Was Clara Mike's girlfriend?

She couldn't be sure. They were certainly friendly and made a fine-looking couple. Her heart sank and suddenly she felt like a foolish little girl. Whatever had given her the idea that there was anything between herself and Mike? It was only her own wishful thinking. How could he ever take any notice of a servant girl? Especially when he was meeting fine young women like Clara every day.

She was relieved when it was time to take her leave and she left with their good wishes for Newport ringing in her ears. How kind they had all been. Then why oh why did she feel so lonesome? Blinking back her tears, she rushed home, determined to forget Mike for once and for all. In her position she had no chance with him at all and never would have. She must put him out of her mind.

The following day dawned bright and sunny. Annie's spirits rose when she and Gertrude were packed into the carriage by Arthur, along with all the luggage, to be driven to Grand Central Station to catch the train north to Newhaven, where they would change for Rhode Island. Arthur would accompany them and he sat atop beside James, the coachman, who would leave them all to the station.

They drew away from the house on Fifth Avenue to the sight of Amy standing alongside Peggy on the front steps waving forlornly until they disappeared from sight.

The train was full and the seats next to them soon filled up, making them appreciate Arthur's insistence on leaving home so early. It seemed everyone in the country was travelling north that day. They pulled out of the huge railway station with its crowds bustling everywhere, harassed parents with anxious faces hurrying to catch trains and over-heated fretful children in tow. Soon they were speeding northwards, leaving a trail of steam behind them.

At Newhaven, Connecticut, they disembarked to change for Rhode Island. They hadn't too long to wait before boarding a smaller, less comfortable train for Newport, and Arthur was hard put to get them seats as the train was already full of passengers, also bound for the seaside port. The girls became more excited as the train followed the coastline, and as they drew into the station at last, they caught the sharp tang of sea air drifting through the open windows.

'There's Old Andy come to meet us,' said Arthur as they stood on the platform surrounded by trunks and boxes and cheerful knots of people greeting each other with cries of delight. The pleasant holiday atmosphere infected Annie and Gertrude and they almost felt that they'd come on holidays themselves as they hopped up on the open car while Old Andy and Arthur busied themselves stowing the luggage away. Within minutes they were trotting briskly down Bellevue Avenue – a fine tree-lined thoroughfare with splendid houses on either side. They then turned left and drove right to the end of Narraganset Avenue, where they drew up before a fine pink stucco villa surrounded on all sides by a wide veranda and a back garden looking out on the ocean. Annie gasped with surprise.

'This is not a cottage.' She turned to Gertrude in amazement. 'It's more like a palace.'

Gertrude, who had been to Newport the previous summer with the family, laughed at Annie's reaction.

'The gentry call them cottages,' she explained.

Annie was overjoyed. What a beautiful place to spend the summer. What a contrast to the enclosed life in the city she'd had all these months. It reminded her of Crosshaven – with its rocky beach stretching out below them. How her little brothers would enjoy this, and her parents and uncle and aunt. She sighed. They'd likely never see it, she knew. Never mind, she would enjoy it and write it all down to tell them.

4
—

A Big Decision

'Amy, Amy,' Annie called, looking around frantically for her young charge. One minute Amy had been nearby, building an elaborate sandcastle, the next minute when Annie looked up from writing in her journal she had disappeared. The beach was crowded. She could be anywhere. This was Easton's – the public beach at Newport, where all but the most exclusive set gathered to enjoy the sand and surf. The Van der Leutens kept to Bailey's Beach, where, as the Mistress put it, you would find no 'riff raff', but Annie, who spent most of her days looking after Amy, preferred Easton's for their daily walk. Amy preferred it too as there were all sorts of amusements and entertainments which you wouldn't find at Bailey's and which she knew her mother probably wouldn't approve of.

Annie hastily gathered up their belongings and ran hurriedly down the beach towards the water, calling out as she went. Suddenly, she saw Amy. She was being swung around and around by a young man. Approaching rapidly, Annie's heart was in her mouth until she saw that it was Robert.

'Master Robert,' she gasped, running up to them, 'I nearly died of the fright. I thought Miss Amy had gone missing. Why ever didn't you tell me where you were off to?' she asked crossly, turning to Amy, who was beaming with delight at having spotted her favourite brother, newly arrived from New York.

'Never mind, Annie,' Robert smiled as she drew level. 'I just got in an hour ago and needed to take a walk. Come on, let's go take one.'

'Oh yes, let's, Robbie. And may Annie come too?' Amy was jumping up and down with excitement.

'Maybe we'd best go back first . . . ' Annie was a bit taken aback by Master Robert's arrival and wondered whether it would be quite proper to take a walk with him and Amy. It might be misunderstood. Master Robert was a young man of her own age after all.

'Nonsense. Let's go. You haven't been here before, Annie, so let me show you some of the sights.' Without even waiting for a reply Robert took her basket and the three of them set off. Annie soon relaxed. Robert was a good guide. They took the cliff walk, which brought them southwards towards Land's End. What a view they had out to sea. The rocky path led along the back gardens of some of the finest of Newport's houses, or mansions as they were called. Robert was able to entertain them with tales of some of the families who lived in them. In turn Annie found herself telling them all about County Cork and the fun they'd had on summer outings to Crosshaven.

'Tell Robbie about the time you all went fishing with

Uncle Charlie, Annie,' begged Amy. 'When Philip fell in the water and nearly drowned.'

'Seems you know Annie's family pretty well,' said Robert, looking at Annie with new interest. 'They sure seem like great people to know.'

'Oh yes, I've been to visit them, and besides, Annie talks about 'em all the time. Don't you, Annie?'

'Whisht now, Miss Amy. We don't want to vex Master Robert now do we and he good enough to take us walking like this.' Annie was embarrassed and wished she had not talked quite so much to Amy about her family. It had been as much to relieve her own loneliness as to amuse Amy that she had done so.

'Go whisht now yourself, Annie, or I'll send you right home this minute,' Robert retorted, taking her off to a T. They all burst out laughing, he sounded so comical. How charming he was, she thought, and a different Robert to the one Annie had seen up to now. The Robert who brought his West Point cadet friends to visit his home in New York had seemed a lot more boisterous and behaved more like the spoilt younger son of wealthy parents. She realised with surprise that he seemed now more like someone of her own age and not just Charles's kid brother. She guessed it was the fact that this was the first time she'd really been in his company in any real sense.

By the time they arrived home for supper, Annie had heard much about Robert's life in West Point, especially the Exhibition Day, which had taken place the previous week and which Amy and his parents had attended.

Amy had already given Annie breathless accounts of

the exploits of Robert's class, which had given a military display in which they – Robbie included – had dug trenches and built defences fit to resist a real cavalry charge, and had followed this with a demonstration of the great new rapid-firing and machine guns.

Robert described it all now in detail, demonstrating his account with vivid actions and sound effects that made Amy and Annie double up with laughter. What fun they had. However, Annie was brought up short when she realised that their afternoon walk had far exceeded the time allotted and that she was expected to be home already, helping Gertrude and the temporary local cook prepare the evening meal.

Over the next few weeks, Annie had many an opportunity to get to know Robert better. Life in Newport was a lot less demanding on the staff, as the Mistress was much taken up with her social activities, which took place largely outside the home. With the Mistress gone for most of the day Annie didn't have the same feeling of being locked away that she had experienced in New York.

She and Gertrude did almost as much housework as they did in New York but were a little more in control of the daily routine with no Mrs Parsons to bite their noses off if they were a minute late with anything and no great amounts of laundry to cope with, as the Mistress sent most of it out to be done locally. Besides, Annie now found she could steal a few moments each day to play the piano – not as fine a one as the family owned in New York but a good one just the same. It was during one of these moments one morning when the Mistress was out that she was surprised by Master Robert. He was standing just inside the parlour door listening while she played some tunes from memory. The sound of clapping made her turn around and there he was.

'Hey, I didn't know you could play,' he said, looking at her in amazement. 'Where did you learn?'

'Oh, Master Robert, you gave me quite a start,' Annie replied, overcome with embarrassment. She hadn't heard him come in. She jumped up from the piano right away.

'No, stay. I want to hear you play some more. It's good to hear someone play the piano. No one ever bothers with it anymore. So you're doing us a favour really. Come on, let's hear you.'

Reluctantly, Annie sat down again and played one or two more melodies softly. She was fretting that someone might come in and disturb them.

But Master Robert sat down quietly nearby. He looked out of the window and seemed to expect her to continue. So she relaxed and lost herself in her playing and forgot about him and where she was. Playing the piano always carried her back in her mind to Cork and the happy times she'd had at the Donohues' house with her friend Julia, play-acting and getting up little entertainments for the family. She no longer fretted for those light-hearted days but she enjoyed remembering them.

As she broke into the old favourite 'Oh My Darling, Clementine' she realised that Robert had joined in, with a pleasant singing voice that she hadn't known he possessed.

'You're a sly one, Annie,' he said as Annie played the last chord and the sound died away. 'I'll wager you can dance too.'

'I can if I've a mind to,' laughed Annie. 'But I haven't had time for it since I've come to America. I'm too busy earning a wage.'

'But why are you doing this kind of work, Annie?' Robert asked, suddenly looking a little uncomfortable. 'I can see you're not cut out to be a servant girl. I mean you do fine at the work but... ' He hesitated, not knowing quite what to say. 'Well, you could do better I'm sure... ' he added lamely.

Annie could see that he really had no idea about her life. He might be clever and make a fine soldier to send out to war but he knew very little else. 'It's not as simple as you think... ' she began hesitantly. But just then she looked through the window and saw the carriage coming up the drive. It was the Mistress returning. 'Look, I cannot talk any more now. I must help Gertrude,' she said, moving hurriedly towards the door. Instinctively she knew that playing the piano and singing with Robert would not meet with the Mistress's approval.

'Will you come bicycling with me, Annie? Do say yes. I want to teach you. All the girls are learning. You'd like it, I know you would.' Robert was at his most persuasive. He caught her hand as she opened the door and held it fast for a moment.

'We could have such fun together,' he added. 'Besides, we're the same age. Amy told me so.' Hearing the carriage door shutting and the Mistress calling something to Andy, Annie pulled her hand away and sped downstairs to the kitchen.

My, what fun it would be to learn how to cycle, she couldn't help thinking as she served lunch to the Mistress, Robert and Amy in the dining room. Women's cycling had become all the rage this summer at Newport and even the Mistress was involved in organising events for the younger society ladies to take part in. There was the Lantern Ride for instance – Annie wished she could have seen it – which by all accounts was a great success. It took place late in the evening with about fifty lady cyclists with lanterns, accompanied by an escort of enthusiasts following in broughams complete with coachmen.

But Annie was to find out before long that Robert was quite in earnest about teaching her to cycle. The very next afternoon when she and Amy were taking their usual stroll to Easton's, Robert turned up with a cycle machine and insisted there and then on giving Annie a lesson. Amy squealed with delight when she saw Annie make her first wobbly efforts with Robert holding the saddle to help her balance. Annie was pleased with herself and felt it wouldn't take too long until she got the hang of it.

That was the first of many lessons that Robert was to give Annie in the art of bicycling over the next few weeks and she was beginning to make such progress that she could now manage quite well on her own without his help, although she still wobbled a lot. By now they had become firm friends and he had insisted that she cease calling him 'Master Robert' and call him 'Robbie' as Amy did.

'At least when we're alone together,' he had said when Annie had at first protested that it wasn't fitting. 'We're friends aren't we?'

Feeling slightly uneasy all the same, Annie decided to ask Gertrude about it when they were sitting quietly in the garden one evening after they had finished their work.

Her friend looked at her thoughtfully before replying. 'There's no harm in it, Annie, of course there's not, but it's not the way things are done and you must know that yourself. If the Mistress were to hear you she would not be too happy, I dare say. We're not gentry you see and Master Robert is. Besides, it could be that he's taken a fancy to you, and where would that get you? I'd be careful if I were in your shoes.'

'Nonsense, Gertrude, he's just like a brother to me,' Annie protested, laughing.

'But you may not be just like a sister to him,' Gertrude retorted quickly, glancing at her friend and remarking once again how very pretty she was. She had noticed how Robert looked at Annie and had formed her own opinion about it. She was anxious not to interfere but she felt increasingly uneasy about the situation.

As it turned out, events took a decisive turn towards the end of that week. Just as Annie was serving the soup at dinner one evening, the Mistress was talking about the latest doings of the Newport Cycling Club, when Amy suggested, 'Perhaps Annie could go with you next time, Mother, now that Robbie has taught her to cycle.'

There was a sudden silence. Annie nearly dropped the soup.

'I beg your pardon, Amy?'

'Why, Mother, Robbie wanted Annie to learn. Nearly every afternoon he brings the bicycle on our walk and . . . '

'Robert, is this true?'

'Why yes, Mother, but where's the harm . . . ?'

'Annie, you may return to the kitchen.'

Annie waited not a moment more but fled, her cheeks scarlet with embarrassment. What had seemed so harm-less she now knew would not be regarded in that light by the Mistress. She was sure to be in trouble. Gertrude took her place and served the rest of the meal to save her friend the embarrassment of having to reappear in the dining room.

'I'll wager she'll be sending for you in a few minutes so tidy yourself up, Annie,' Gertrude confided in whispers when she returned after serving the main course.

Sure enough, Annie hadn't long to wait before she was summoned to the parlour. This was her second encounter with the Mistress in an angry mood and she felt sure she would be sent packing. But strangely, it wasn't quite as she had predicted. The Mistress was firm but her tone of voice was kind enough.

'I understand from my son, Annie, that he saw fit to teach you how to bicycle. That was very kind of him but misplaced. He is young and doesn't yet know his place in society. He will not bother you again, never fear. You must not think ill of him. He means well. Now you may return to your work. I have kept you too much from it. I shall take charge of Amy for the remainder of our time here.'

Annie left feeling confused and somehow uneasy. She had not been sent packing. That was good but somehow she felt she had been misjudged or the situation had been misconstrued. Amy crept into the kitchen later and said she was sorry for it all and that her Mama was sending Robbie back to New York to work for her Papa. When pressed further, Amy revealed that Robbie had been severely chastised for 'mixing with the servants'.

Annie was mortified but her first reaction was to comfort poor Amy, who was close to tears. She wound her arms around Annie's neck, whispering, 'I'm sorry, Annie, it's all my fault.'

'Of course it's not, pet. No one has done any harm, never you fear,' Annie reassured her.

Sure enough, by the next morning Robert had been dispatched. By this time Annie had had time to think about what had happened and knew instinctively that she had misjudged the situation from the start. She was simply not the social equal of Robert and there was no question of their being friends. She was a servant girl and he was the son of her wealthy employers. As Gertrude had pointed out, it simply wasn't done. She also knew that this was something the Mistress would not forget, for all that she had not treated her harshly over it. Annie had committed the cardinal error of not knowing her place. She would be watched.

No more was said about the matter. Their stay at Newport resumed its pleasant rhythm, the Mistress soon tiring of an excess of Amy's company and leaving her again mostly in Annie and Gertrude's charge. In

fact, the Mistress began to make use of Annie's assist-
ance to typewrite her correspondence more and more,
which was helpful in developing Annie's skill. But
somehow, Annie felt a great change in her attitude
towards her work with the family. She no longer valued
it as much as she had. It wasn't just that her pride had
been hurt. Yes, she felt belittled but she also felt
contempt for the Mistress's attitude and quietly resolved to leave the service of the Van der Leutens as
soon as she could.

*

Having more time on her hands than she had had when
working in New York, Annie had time to think about
what she would do. Father and Mother would be angry
with her, she knew, were she to leave the Van der
Leutens without good reason. She knew her parents
would not consider this incident good reason. Nor was
it, in truth, but she could not quite explain, even to
herself, her sudden distaste for continuing in their
service. But what could she do? She had not learned
enough at night-school to land a job as a clerk. Perhaps
Mike could help her out once again. No, she was uncomfortable about asking for Mike's help. She had not
discovered whether he was walking out with Clara
Stevenson or not, and deep down she didn't want to
know. She had written to Molly and had received letters
from her since she had come to Newport but both girls
had avoided mentioning the subject. No doubt she
would find out in due course.

Constantly in the company of Gertrude, she began to like and respect her friend more and more and one evening as they talked, an idea struck her.

'When are you returning to Nebraska, Gertrude?' she asked suddenly.

'I hope to travel home for Thanksgiving, and then Eric and I will be married next summer,' Gertrude replied happily, always pleased to speak of her plans for the future. She had quite a bit of money put away by now and longed to return to her fiancé and her family.

'Do you think you'd like a companion on the journey?' asked Annie, smiling mischievously.

'You want to come to Nebraska, Annie? Truly?' Gertrude was astounded, her eyes as round as saucers.

'Yes, I think I do. I've promised my friend Ellie King many times that I will visit her some day and I think that day has come,' Annie replied, quite serious now. 'It's been in the back of my mind for a long time.'

What plans were made that night! The two girls sharing the attic bedroom didn't get to sleep until very late, planning and discussing what they might do, when they might travel, what kind of work Annie might get in Nebraska.

Writing to Ellen the very next day, Annie felt sure that a new phase in her life was about to begin.

5

Breaking the News

Annie's plans to accompany Gertrude to Nebraska had progressed considerably since their return from Rhode Island to New York. She had received a delighted letter from Ellen King, assuring her that she would be welcomed with open arms. 'I long to see you again,' wrote Ellen. 'I would love you to meet Dan and be here when my baby comes.' She had expected as much, as Ellen always asked in her letters when Annie might travel west.

'You will find life here hard at first,' Ellen continued 'and different to anywhere you've lived before. The past year was the toughest yet, with the terrible drought, but they say it is set to improve for next year. The winters are hard too but it's a great place to live all the same and I've grown to love it.'

Annie knew that her hardest task would be to confront her parents and let them know of her decision. It was something she must do as soon as possible if she intended to give in her notice to the Van der Leutens and be ready to travel with Gertrude at the end of November.

Her opportunity came the very next Sunday when she visited Monroe Street to find only her mother and father at home, the boys having gone off with Uncle Charlie. After an enthusiastic welcome and exclamations of delight at how well she looked, Annie knew she had to tell them right then and there.

'Father, Mother, look I've something to say. Sit down will you. We must have a talk.'

Seeing the serious look on their daughter's face, Matt and Mary exchanged concerned glances and sat down.

'What's troubling you, alannah?' her father asked.

'I'm going to be giving notice at the Van der Leutens,' she began. There was a shocked gasp from her mother; her father just narrowed his eyes. Annie knew that look. Her heart sank but she continued to speak, not meeting his eye but looking at a spot on the wall between the two of them. It all came out in a rush.

'I know you won't be happy about it and I know it's a good position I'm leaving but I don't want to be a servant girl all my life. I plan to leave in November and go out to Nebraska with Gertrude. She's going home to marry and I'm going to stay with Ellie King. Ellie says there's lots of work out there if you're strong and able-bodied. She says . . . '

'I don't care what she says,' thundered Father. 'Are you mad, girl? You'll be throwing everything away if you go out there.' He was spitting out the words. 'Is that what we brought you out from Ireland for? To throw it all away just when you're beginning to do well. To throw it all away on this . . . this . . . foolhardy plan.'

Mother was now crying softly into her apron.

'Mother, please don't upset yourself. I'll be perfectly safe. I have always said I would like to see more of America. This is a good chance for me, truly it is.'

'And what work do you think you will get out in the wilds. Is it as a cattle hand you'll end up? In the name of God, girl, is it mad you are?' Father was now red in the face with rage.

'I've thought about it for a long time, Father. I really want to go. Ellie says there are lots of opportunities out there. Please don't be angry. I must do something more with my life. I've saved money which will get me through until I find work.'

But Father was adamant. It would be the ruin of her. She'd live to regret it. She needn't think she could come crawling back home. If she went she could stay there for all he cared. She escaped as quickly as she could, his words echoing in her ears as she ran down the stairs. Annie was upset at the vehemence of her father's outburst, but by now she was so determined to go that nothing would have changed her mind.

As she reached the end of Monroe Street it suddenly occurred to her that she hadn't seen the Rostovs for a long time. She might be lucky enough to catch Sophia at home. Annie knew that her friend would understand her dilemma. She was in luck. Sophia was on a day's leave from the hospital and was alone in the apartment.

'Annie, what a wonderful surprise!'

What a pleasure it was to see Sophia again. They rarely found an opportunity these days to meet, what with both of them having so few days off and seldom at the same time. Sophia was soon pouring cups of steaming hot tea from the samovar and Annie needed no second invitation to sample some of Mama Rostov's famous little iced cakes. Sophia listened attentively as her friend poured out her hopes and plans for a new life in the wide open spaces of the West, a place she could not even visualise, yet which Annie, from her many talks with Gertrude and letters from Ellen, could describe in detail.

'It's like a new land, Sophia. It's been a new start for so many people. Women can get work there just like the men. It's hard I know, but it's a great adventure. Why don't my parents understand that?'

'Because they're not young, Annie, like us,' her friend said thoughtfully. 'Because they have had their great adventure – coming to America. Do you not understand?'

While Sophia was surprised at Annie's news she was not shocked. She knew that Annie was not and never would be happy to continue working as a servant girl. Like Molly, Sophia saw that work of that nature would never be enough for her friend.

Annie walked homewards to Fifth Avenue later that balmy September evening, comforted by her talk with Sophia but still angry with her father and saddened at having upset her mother. She knew she would not be able to see them again until next week but perhaps it was just as well. They might have come around to her way of thinking by then. She was committed to going now and would shortly give her notice to the Van der Leutens. They would not be pleased either, no doubt, but not because they would be concerned about her, like her parents, but because it simply would not suit them to lose two staff at the same time. She knew Amy would be particularly upset and that would be something she'd have to deal with too.

Then she thought about Mike and for the umpteenth time she wondered about him and Clara. She had not contacted Molly since she'd returned to New York and deep down she knew that she was afraid to hear that perhaps Mike and Clara were sweethearts. She would so dearly like to see him again, just once, before she went away. She vowed to write a note to Molly and arrange to meet as soon as possible. Her friend did not even know of her plans.

The very next morning she received a note from Molly chiding her for her tardiness and requesting a meeting as soon as possible. Annie posted off her reply later the same day, arranging to meet Molly on her next evening off.

*

It came as something of a shock when she arrived at the tea rooms at the agreed time on Thursday evening to find not Molly but Mike waiting for her. Although her first reaction as she walked towards him was one of delight, it then struck her that perhaps he was there to meet someone else and then, when she saw him beckoning to her, that something serious had brought him here.

'Mike, has something happened?'

'Annie, how good to see you again.' Mike sounded a

little strained, Annie thought instantly. 'No, no, of course not,' he added, seeing how taken aback she was. He had shaken her hand in a formal way and then stood back to let her pass through the door ahead of him.

'Are you alone then?' More and more curious, Annie followed him as he led the way to a table in the corner. 'I was to meet Molly. Is she . . . ?'

'She cannot come, I'm afraid,' Mike replied. But he did not explain why. He seemed to be avoiding her eye. He busied himself ordering tea and then he looked at her and started to speak.

'Annie, I believe you plan to go out west shortly.'

'Yes, Mike, it is true. But how did you . . . ?'

But Mike did not let her finish. Looking embarrassed, he hesitated, then spoke. 'Annie, I'm here because your parents are troubled about you and they asked me to come and see you and try and persuade you not to go ahead with this plan.'

'You're here because my parents sent you?'

'They didn't exactly send me, but they asked my advice and I offered to come along and have a talk with you about it.'

'What?' Annie looked aghast. Then she became angry. She flushed with annoyance. How dare her parents go seeking advice for her problems. How dare Mike come here prepared to lecture her in place of her father.

In an icy tone of voice, she said, 'Mike, I am no longer a child and I don't wish to be treated like one. I don't know what my parents have told you but I earn my own living, I am nearly eighteen years old and I do not need such advice as you can give me. Especially as it is probably my parents' advice.' She stood up. 'I see now why you've come. Please do not fret on my account, Mike, because I shall go to Nebraska no matter what.'

Mike had lost his embarrassed look. He was looking at her as if he was really seeing her for the first time. He seemed upset.

'Annie, Annie, please, I'm sorry . . . I didn't mean . . . You know I feel responsible for you somehow since we first met. I care about what happens to you. Truly, Annie . . . '

But Annie had donned her cloak. She gave him a withering look. 'Responsible for me, is it? Mike, nobody is responsible for me but myself. I have my own life to live and I will do so, without help from you or anyone else.'

Furious now, Annie turned on her heel and swept out of the tea-rooms, leaving Mike looking after her in amazement. She ran down the street, tears of anger and disappointment springing up in her eyes. When she had got far enough away to be able to pause for a moment without fear of being seen, she stopped to catch her breath. Responsible for her. She'd soon show him. Cares about what happens to her. That's not the way a man would feel if he was even halfway in love with her. He sounded like her brother Tom. That was it in a nutshell. He didn't love her, of course he didn't. Why did she keep fooling herself? Annie felt as if all her dreams were shattering around her like pieces of broken glass.

Somehow she got home and, thankfully, met no one on the stairs as she ran up to her room. Throwing herself on her bed, she wept as if her heart would break. In some way the decision to go to Nebraska had changed everything, isolating her from all the people she loved. Could she go ahead with it? Was it the right decision?

Next morning when she awoke the sun was shining straight in the window and somehow things didn't seem quite so bad. As she dressed Annie felt sure that her decision was the right one. Now she was sure there was nothing more for her in New York and that Nebraska offered everything – a great adventure, a chance to make a new life, meet new people, learn new ways. She would bring her parents around somehow.

She was anxious now about how the Mistress would react as they had had cross words again recently and Annie judged it would be best to postpone giving in her notice for the moment. One month's advance warning was all she was required to give after all, so she hoped to get back in the Mistress's good books first.

Their latest conflict had been about pay. In recent times Annie had made herself very useful to the Mistress with her new skill at typewriting as well as her ability to look after and occupy Amy. However, when she had looked for a small raise in pay for the extra work, the Mistress had refused outright, reminding her firmly yet again of her place in the household.

'I cannot afford to pay my servants any more than I am paying already,' she had replied frostily on that occasion. Annie, knowing how much more a stenographer would be paid in a city business house, felt aggrieved at the Mistress's refusal to grant her even a little extra. After all, it wasn't as if her household duties were cut down to compensate. She must still complete all of those.

Annie had still not seen Molly, and, determined to have a reunion with her and share all her plans, she wrote her a note suggesting they make another attempt to meet in the coming week. 'I will await you at the usual place at seven o'clock. Please come this time. I need to talk to you.' She still didn't know precisely what had happened to prevent her friend from coming on the last occasion. She assumed that Mike had told her of his talk with Annie's parents, or perhaps Tom had told her and she had agreed to let Mike come in her place.

Annie knew that discussing all of this with Molly would be painful now that she had quarrelled with Mike, and she knew it would inevitably be mentioned. But she couldn't leave New York without saying good-bye to Molly. Apart from Sophia, Molly was the best friend she had here. Molly had kept in contact with her even though Annie's work hours made it difficult and inconvenient for her to do so. She had encouraged her to go to night school and in every way she had been an important link for Annie to the world outside the Van der Leutens.

She need have had no worries. Molly greeted her with outstretched hands, almost unable to contain her excitement.

'Annie, I could hardly wait to see you when I heard your news. How I wish I was going with you. Quickly, tell me all about it.'

'And how do you know I have anything to tell you,

Miss Busybody,' Annie joked, much relieved.

'Mike told Tom and Tom told me,' Molly replied.

This time the two friends had no interruptions and Annie confided her plans, delighted that Molly was so enthusiastic. She felt more and more confident that she was doing the right thing.

'So you see it's well-planned, Molly, and not foolhardy as Father seems to think. And I suppose you've only heard ill of me from Mike,' Annie concluded, glancing anxiously at her friend.

'No, Annie, not at all. I haven't spoken with Mike about it. Tom says he has been very quiet about it.'

Then Annie, seeing her friend's sympathetic expression, confessed how angry she had been with him and how confused she was.

'I fear Mike doesn't feel for me what I do for him, Moll,' she said finally in a low, defeated voice.

'Annie, I don't know Mike very well and I can't say I know what he feels but I know he is very fond of you,' Molly replied sympathetically.

'Is he ... I mean is Clara ... you know that girl I met with him last time here ... are they ... ?' Annie hardly knew how to ask. Molly knew she had to be honest with her friend.

'Yes, Annie, they are walking out together, if that's what you mean,' she replied.

'So they are not betrothed then?' Annie asked.

'Certainly they are not betrothed, Annie, but I believe they do see quite a lot of one another.'

Annie had to be content with that. On reflection, she felt sorry about how she had behaved to him. He had been put in an awkward position by her parents and had been as embarrassed as she was angry. Annie now realised that it was mostly her own pride that had made her react as she had.

6

DISGRACED!

During the month of October, Annie and Gertrude spent every minute they could spare from their work preparing for their trip west. The matter of Gertrude giving notice to the family was only a matter of form as they had known for some time that she would be departing in November. Nothing, however, could have prepared Annie for the fuss the Mistress would kick up when she handed in her notice in mid-October, five weeks before their planned departure date.

'I consider it very ungrateful of you, Annie,' she remonstrated. 'After the trouble I've taken with you. Besides, what will Amy do? I cannot leave her in Peggy's charge. It's most unkind of you to walk off . . . and with Gertrude too. And as if that weren't enough you're going off just before Thanksgiving. How will Cook manage?'

Annie, listening to this tirade, longed to reply that she'd just have to hire someone else but knew that would get her into trouble so she hung her head, trying to look guilty. The Mistress knew right well she could hire replacements for herself and Gertrude tomorrow. She just didn't want to have the trouble of it. It was right generous of me to give her over a month's notice, Annie thought to herself, many a parlourmaid would have only given a week.

But it was Amy who really did manage to make Annie feel bad when the news came out. She was inconsolable.

'Why can't you take me with you? I want to go and see Ellen and the new baby,' she wailed. 'And I want to visit with Gertrude's family. Don't leave me behind, Annie, please don't.'

'But, alannah, the baby isn't even born yet,' Annie soothed. 'Besides, what would your poor mother do all alone here without you?'

'She doesn't need me . . . '

'Yes she does and Robert needs you. What would he do if he arrived home and found you gone?'

But there was nothing Annie could say right then to make it all right with the little girl. Trying to console her as best she could, she reflected guiltily once more on how she had upset everyone with her plans. However, with the promise of regular letters describing her new life in the West, Amy was somewhat mollified.

At least Annie's parents were now resigned to her plan, which was a comfort, although she was still at a loss as to how or why they had changed their minds. She suspected Mike had something to do with it. She didn't dare ask.

The next few weeks passed quickly, with a flurry of letters between New York and Nebraska as the final

details of the trip west were settled. The two girls'
excitement infected the rest of the staff at the Van der
Leutens and everyone contributed advice on the adventure. Even Cook had something to add, suggesting they
bring their favourite sweetmeats from New York as they
would get no such luxuries out west.

It came as something of a surprise to Annie during
this period when Robert arrived home for a weekend.
She had understood he would not be returning until
Thanksgiving, by which time she would be in Nebraska.
Although she was a little nervous about seeing him
again she kept telling herself that she had nothing to
be ashamed of. However, she also resolved to behave
in an appropriate fashion when she did meet him and
hoped he would do the same and not address her in
the familiar manner he had used while in Newport.

As it turned out, she didn't see him until the Sunday,
her day off. As she mounted the stairs to her room on
her return late that evening she encountered him,
sitting on the bottom step of the narrow staircase
leading to the servants' quarters in the attic. He jumped
to his feet the moment she appeared, leaving her in no
doubt that he had been waiting for her.

'Robbie, what are you doing here,' whispered Annie,
dismayed enough to forget her resolution to address
him more formally.

'I had to see you, Annie, just once before you go,'
he replied, leaning forward to shut the door, closing
them off from the family's living quarters.

'But I can't talk to you here, you know that.' Feeling
very ill at ease, Annie tried to push past him on the

staircase. But he barred her way.

'You never told me you were going away so I came back to see you. Let's go up to your room and we can talk some more. You are so beautiful, Annie, I can't stop thinking about you. I know you feel the same way.'

Suddenly Annie was scared. Robbie had a look on his face that she had never seen before and she found it unnerving. The smiling, charming manner was gone and in its place was a look of ruthless determination that made him seem like a different person.

'Please let me pass. You know you cannot come up to my room. I will be the one in trouble if . . . '

'Not so fast . . . you'll be in trouble if you don't say goodbye to me the way I want.'

At this, he caught her to him roughly. Struggling to free herself Annie only succeeded in making him hold her in an even tighter grip. Suddenly, the door at the bottom of the stairs opened and the appalled voice of Mrs Van der Leuten broke in on the scene.

'What is the meaning of this?'

Robert had released his hold on Annie instantly and sprung back, leaving her to fall backwards against the banisters in complete disarray. He took charge of the situation immediately.

'Mother, I am sorry to disturb you,' he said in a calm, smooth voice, 'but Annie asked me to visit her in her room – I didn't know to what purpose – and now I find she wishes to bid me farewell.'

Annie could not believe her ears.

'But Ma'am, it's not true. I did no such thing, Ma'am please believe me. He was waiting here when I . . . '

The Mistress cut her off with a peremptory gesture and addressed her son. 'Robert, go to your room – I will speak to you later.' She stood back to let him pass through the door. Then, turning to Annie, she looked her up and down with ill-concealed contempt. Annie was in a mess. Her hair had come loose and had fallen down in an untidy heap about her shoulders, her hat lay where it had fallen on the floor, the sleeve of her dress was torn just under the armpit and her face was red from both shock and embarrassment.

'As for you, Annie Moore, I've suspected all along that you would prove a bad influence. Pray God you have not contaminated Amy with your wickedness. You may leave this house first thing tomorrow morning and never let me see you under my roof again.'

Before Annie could reply, the Mistress turned on her heel and swept through the door, pulling it shut behind her.

Annie sat down on the stairs with a thud. She felt dazed and could hardly believe what had just taken place. Everything had been going so well, she thought. Now, suddenly and without warning, she was in total disgrace. Dismissed from her job. A failure. And Robert? How she had been deceived! How could he have behaved like that? How could he treat her in such a brutal way and then blame the whole thing on her? He had got her sacked. There was no doubt about that. Now she was without a job and would not have enough saved for her trip west. She needed to earn that money over the next month and in an instant he had deprived her of it.

How wrong she had been about him. Gertrude had been right to warn her when they were in Newport but of course she had not heeded her friend. What a stupid fool she had been. With this the tears came and, gathering herself together, she wearily climbed the steep narrow stairs to her attic room for the last time. She spoke to no one and even though she knew Gertrude would be in her room on the same corridor and probably still awake she couldn't face her and decided she would write a note to her friend instead, explaining what had happened, and slip it under her door first thing tomorrow before she left.

Annie had little sleep that night. She went over the scene in her mind again and again, trying to detect any fault on her side. Had she encouraged him in any way? How could he have misunderstood her so badly? But try as she would to account for Robert's behaviour, she came to the conclusion that she had never regarded him other than as a friend and had never, she thought, given him reason to think she had regarded him in any other way. Why oh why had she not listened to Gertrude? And now she would have to face her parents. The prospect of her father's wrath was too much for Annie to bear and she broke down again in sobs. She just could not go back to Monroe Street. Whatever about Mother, she knew that Father would not believe her story.

Rising before anyone – even the servants – had stirred, Annie tiptoed down the stairs and left the Van der Leutens' fine house by the servants' entrance, carrying her trunk, which she had packed some hours earlier before falling into a brief, uneasy sleep.

It wasn't until she had walked some hundred yards or so down Fifth Avenue and was well clear of the house that she gave any thought as to where she would go now. All she wanted to do was to get away without having to see anyone, especially Robert. She had written a note to Gertrude. And Amy. How could she explain to the child why she was leaving in such a stealthy manner? She didn't care what the others thought. Let Mrs Van der Leuten explain it how she chose. It made no difference to her; what she said would be untrue in any case.

She stood pondering what she should do. She could not go to her parents in Monroe Street. How about Tom? Surely he would understand. He had been in a fair bit of trouble a couple of years ago and she had helped him. But no, if she went to him she would have to confront Mike and that would be unthinkable. Molly would be sympathetic but she lived with her family in Brooklyn. No, that wasn't a possibility either. It was cold and pitch dark and there were few people about. Annie shivered. She felt fearful and very alone. She had better not stay here for long. God knows what kind of ne'er-do-wells would be about at this hour.

Then suddenly it came to her. Auntie Norah! Why hadn't she thought of her straightaway? Auntie Norah would surely understand and take her part. Yes, she would go there directly. If she could pick up a horse cab she should just get there before Auntie Norah left for her work in the city store. Uncle Charlie would already be on his way to the Fulton Market, as he started work at dawn.

By the time Annie arrived at Auntie Norah's it was beginning to get brighter and people were about. She felt her spirits rising as she mounted the stairs of the tenement house where they lived in Cherry Street. Thank God, Auntie Norah was still at home and promptly answered her knock on the door.

'God save us, Annie, what are you doing here, child, at this hour? I'm just about to leave for work. Are you all right? Come in, come in.'

Annie lugged her trunk inside and shut the door. Collapsing on the nearest chair she quickly told her aunt the whole story. When she had finished, a silence fell. Auntie Norah had her face averted and she did not look one bit happy. Annie had a sinking feeling suddenly in the pit of her stomach. If Auntie Norah didn't believe her, what chance had she with her father.

'It doesn't seem to me, Annie, that you have behaved very wisely in this whole affair,' said Auntie Norah finally. 'How could this young man have been on those kind of terms with you in the first place?'

'I told you, Auntie Norah, we were friends, just friends. It was while I was away in Newport. He taught me to bicycle and we became friends. That's all. I promise.'

'But lord sakes, Annie, you can't be friends with someone of his ilk, you must know that. Look, I must leave now or I'll be late. Stay here if you wish until I return this evening and we'll talk about it but please understand I can't be taking your side against the family or anything like that so please don't expect it.'

With that she was gone and Annie was left alone to

face this new setback. This was not what she had expected of Auntie Norah. It seemed everyone was against her, she thought wearily. Suddenly it all seemed too much and she was grateful just to lie down on the daybed in Auntie Norah's kitchen. Within minutes she had fallen fast asleep.

When Annie awoke at noon, she didn't know where she was at first. Then it all came flooding back. She remembered Norah's critical words earlier that morning. Slowly it dawned on her that she couldn't hide out here indefinitely. At some stage she was going to have to face her parents and explain what had happened. Perhaps she could tell them she had left early in order to prepare for her trip to Nebraska. After all she had already given in her notice so strictly speaking she hadn't really been sacked. Dismissed, yes, but she need not tell them that in so many words. But they would know well that for all that she had her savings, she couldn't afford four weeks off work without pay.

As she made herself something to eat she gradually came to the bleak conclusion that the only thing she could do was to speak to her parents. She would go to Monroe Street directly. At least she would have an opportunity to speak privately with her mother before the boys returned from school and her father returned from work. It would be far worse for her should she try to tell her news in front of the whole family.

'Annie, why are you not at work?' Her mother was astounded to see her daughter on a Monday afternoon, having parted from her only the night before and not having any expectation of seeing her again until the following Sunday. 'Is there something wrong?'

She could see by her daughter's face that there was indeed something wrong and drew her into the apartment, quickly shutting the door in the face of curious looks from her next-door neighbour Mrs Petrowski.

'I no longer have any work to be doing, Mother,' Annie replied in a low voice, feeling the tears well up again as she saw her mother's anxious expression. 'I've been dismissed.'

When Annie looked back at that day, she remembered it as one of the worst she'd ever spent. First of all there was her mother's bitterly disappointed reaction. That had almost upset her more than the anger her father showed later that evening when he returned, and he was very angry indeed.

'You're a spoiled, slothful girl,' he railed. 'See where your fancy notions of grandeur have got you? It's not good enough for you to land a decent job with the quality but you have to go thinking you're as good as them. Well, listen to me my girl, you would do well to remember you come from a decent family, as decent as ever was and now you've gone and brought disgrace upon us. Hobnobbing with the likes of that young man. You're lucky you were caught early, I tell you, or you could have got yourself into serious trouble, believe me.'

'But I told you, Father, I told you I did nothing wrong only be friendly . . . ' Annie lifted a tear-stained face to her father, who was now pacing up and down the small living-room like a caged tiger. Mother sat in the corner with her hands over her face and the boys cowered in the bedroom.

'Friendly is it?' her father bellowed. 'What call have you to become friends with your employer's son? It's not your place to become friendly. It's your place to work, do you hear me? Work is the only thing that gets you places in America, not friendliness. You see now where friendliness has got you. You've gone and disgraced us, so you have. You'll not get another job now.'

Auntie Norah called a little later and it was finally decided that Annie should stay with her and Charlie for the time being as they had more space. Annie also had to promise her mother to call to Sister Bonaventure the very next day and explain what had happened. She at least owed her that much.

And so it was a very heavy-hearted Annie who finally climbed into Auntie Norah's extra little bed later that night. The only kind word she'd had in the entire day was from Uncle Charlie, who, when she arrived back with Norah, handed her a cup of hot milk and said softly, 'Down that girl, 'twill do you good.'

Annie dreaded her interview with Sister Bonventure, fearing that Mrs Van der Leuten would have already told her the whole story. However, she saw straightaway when she entered the convent parlour that no such event had taken place, as Sister Bonaventure greeted her smilingly. But as Annie told her tale she could see the nun's face becoming stiff with disapproval and a heavy silence fell when she had finished.

'I would never have recommended you for that post had I thought you would behave in this way,' she said eventually. 'It seems you aren't suited to a position with a family. I can do nothing for you now, I'm afraid,' she added, shaking her head.

Annie's apologies fell on deaf ears. There was no persuading Sister Bonaventure that she was not at fault in this matter. As a downhearted Annie left the convent she reflected that indeed everyone she had told about her dismissal had reacted the same way. No matter that Robert had lied, no matter that he had roughly abused her, no matter that Mrs Van der Leuten had not listened to her explanation – in the end it all came down to the fact that she had befriended him. In doing that she had put herself on an equal footing with him – in other words she had not known her place. Annie had learnt a bitter lesson.

7

UNCLE CHARLIE TO THE RESCUE

Annie's one fear in the days following her dismissal from the Van der Leutens' was that her parents would raise fresh objections to her plans to travel west with Gertrude in a month's time. She was grateful to be staying with Charlie and Norah as there would be less opportunity to argue with her father. Although she was still seething with anger over the unjust treatment she had received from the Van der Leutens she was nonetheless very chastened by the whole experience, especially by the way her family had reacted. Nonetheless, she was still determined to go ahead with her travel plans and with this in mind wrote a note to Gertrude telling her where she was staying and asking that they meet on Gertrude's day off. Gertrude replied by return of post a warm, sympathetic letter that brought tears to Annie's eyes. She had been fearful that her friend might not have seen her side of the story.

'You are well off out of here, Annie, as things are going from bad to worse now with the Mistress in a temper because she has to stay home and look after

Amy,' wrote Gertrude. 'Your disappearance caused a lot of talk in the kitchen but nobody really believed that you were the one at fault.' She ended by suggesting a time and place for them to meet and discuss their travel plans.

Reassured somewhat, Annie turned her mind to thinking what she might do to earn some money over the next month. As soon as she mentioned it one evening, Uncle Charlie said, 'Why don't you come along down to the Fish Market with me tomorrow and we'll see if we can get you some work. It's the busiest time of year coming up to Thanksgiving and I'm sure someone could do with help on the stalls.'

Although Annie secretly thought she'd rather go back to laundry work than set off for the Fish Market before dawn, she decided she was in no position to turn down Uncle Charlie's offer without at least giving it a try. He had been the only one in the family who had not scolded or criticised her over her trouble and his unerring good humour had even brought Auntie Norah around to see that maybe Annie's losing her job was not the end of the world and perhaps not even entirely her own fault.

'Why yes, Uncle Charlie, I'll come with you tomorrow then,' Annie replied.

'Then we'll have twice the amount of fish to eat,' smiled Auntie Norah, obviously pleased at Annie's cheerful acceptance of the offer. One good thing about Uncle Charlie's job in the Fish Market was that he came home with all the fish they could eat and it cost him next to nothing. It meant quite a saving on food and he often had enough to pass on to the family at Monroe Street as well as to their own next-door neighbours in Cherry Street.

She and Uncle Charlie set off at four-thirty the next morning, passing under the great Brooklyn Bridge on their way to the East River waterfront. It was still pitch dark and Annie was glad she had Uncle Charlie to accompany her. If she thought the Fulton Fish Market would be a dark, deserted spot before dawn she was in for a big surprise. It seemed like half the population of New York was there when they arrived, shortly before five o'clock.

Annie was astounded at the scene of hectic activity that met her eyes. A fleet of fishing boats was unloading its cargo at the landing slip, and the creels of fresh fish were brought straight to the market to be auctioned and sold on to restaurants, bars and retail stores throughout the city. A huge variety of both freshwater and saltwater fish from as far away as Canada and North Carolina could be bought here, explained Uncle Charlie. Oysters were among the most popular things on sale and already crowds of people gathered around the oyster stand, where Charlie worked with Ned Murphy.

'Take a look around yourself, Annie,' suggested Charlie, 'and I'll have a word with Ned to see if he might know of any work for you.'

Annie set off to explore the huge terracotta building and had to take care not to get lost among the maze of stalls already thronged with potential buyers. To watch the huge crates of fish being weighed on giant scales before being auctioned off was the most amazing sight of all. The speed of it took her breath away and she marvelled at the way the auctioneer standing on a wooden platform above the crowd was able to reel off the names of all those fish without once slipping up. And as for the buyers – you'd want to be quick off the mark to get what you wanted. As she returned to the oyster stand she saw Uncle Charlie beckoning to her.

'I think I have something for you, lass,' he said, introducing her to Ned, who, giving her a quick approving glance, said, 'Yes, you'll do, you look smart enough for it,' and without a second's delay led her back the way she had come, over to where the auctions were taking place.

'I've an extra runner for you, Billy,' he said to the clerk in one of the offices behind the platform, and left to return to his work without a word of explanation.

What could he mean, Annie wondered with dismay, having not the faintest idea of what a 'runner' was expected to do. However, she hadn't a moment to think about it as Billy lined her up with a number of other young people of around her own age standing at the base of the platform.

'Watch what the others do. As soon as a bid is agreed, the auctioneer writes down the price on the docket. You have to take the docket and run and give it to the client who made the bid. You have to make sure to give it to the right person, so when it's your turn you need to climb up on the stand beside the auctioneer, watch the bidding and see exactly who has made the winning bid. And be snappy about it. Okay?'

These instructions were delivered at almost the same speed as the auctioneer was auctioning off the fish.

Annie needed no further explanation as she heard the mallet thumping down on the table as a bid was concluded and within seconds a boy of about sixteen shot down the steps of the platform and ran past them at full speed and into the crowd. Thankfully there were three other runners to go before it was her turn. She noticed the others looking at her with curiosity – she was the only girl – and hoped they wouldn't make any remarks. She could be as good as any of them.

Then it was her turn to climb the steps to the platform. Her appearance caused a bit of a stir – the crowd had obviously never seen a girl do the job – as she took her place beside the auctioneer, who was opening the bidding for a barrel of halibut. There was a laugh from the crowd as some wit remarked, 'You caught yourself a fine fish there, Frank,' but Annie, though inwardly mortified, ignored them and concentrated on the bidding. She watched closely and saw a portly gentleman near the back of the crowd raise his hand each time in response as the bidding rose.

'Going, going, gone to Delmonico's,' cried the auctioneer as his mallet came down with a thump. Instantly, a blue docket was thrust into her hand and she was off, down the steps and running to where she had seen the winning bidder. Luckily, he was quite distinctive-looking and was standing right at the back. She handed him the docket. So far, so good.

And so it went on. Right through the morning she ran hither and thither for the auctioneer, carrying dockets to the clients and trying not to get confused. But she managed well enough and was gratified at the end of the morning's work to be told she would be hired again the following morning. Uncle Charlie was pleased too and made sure she had something to eat at his stand at lunchtime.

'Good girl. It's not everyone who makes a runner, I can tell you,' he said proudly. 'And I haven't seen many girls make a go of it.'

Annie spent the afternoon helping Uncle Charlie on his stand until at last it was time to go home. She got fifty cents at the end of the day for her work as a runner and a dime from Ned for helping on the stand. Although it didn't compare to the kind of money she had been earning at the Van der Leutens, and it was hard work, she was grateful for it.

To her surprise Annie became quite good at the work and was hired every day from then on. She would at least have a little more saved against her trip. At the end of the first week, Uncle Charlie made a visit to Monroe Street and reported her success.

'Give the lass a chance, Matt,' he said. 'She's a good girl and a grand worker. Just because she got on the wrong side of that bounder doesn't mean she's a bad 'un. She's right sorry for what happened and has learned her lesson. She won't make the same mistake again.'

'Mmm, perhaps you're right,' said Annie's father, sucking on his pipe. 'She'd better not. Her trouble is she's always been too big for her boots.'

'Well now and that's not always a bad thing,' replied

Uncle Charlie, never one to give up when it came to making the peace. 'You'd need to be able to fill 'em here or you'd get no place.'

*

When Annie plucked up the courage to visit her family a few days later, she found to her great relief that the way had been somewhat smoothed for her and it seemed she had been forgiven at last. At least there were no arguments. Nor was anything said about her trip to Nebraska, which was now only two weeks away. Gradually, things returned to normal. With Uncle Charlie around, no one could stay angry for long and by the end of the second week, Annie's relationship with her parents had, to her great relief, returned to normal.

She and Gertrude met to finalise their plans and book their train tickets to the West. They would leave New York from Grand Central Station on Forty-second Street on a Saturday afternoon at 4.30 aboard the New York–Chicago Limited Daily Mail. The Empire State Express – the fastest train in the world, according to Uncle Charlie – had proved just too expensive for their modest pockets. They would make stops at Cleveland and Detroit before arriving in Chicago the following afternoon at 5.30. There they would catch the night sleeper west to Omaha, Nebraska, where they would be met by Gertrude's family, with whom Annie was to stay until after Thanksgiving. She would then travel on further westwards to Kimball, to be met by Ellen and

Dan, who would drive her some fifty miles to their prairie home.

'Be sure to bring your warmest garments,' Ellen had written. 'The winters here are much, much colder than New York and will stay so until next May.'

Thanks to Gertrude, Annie was well prepared for the Nebraska winter. The two girls managed to go shopping together on the last Sunday before their departure and had a marvellous time hunting down extra-warm clothing at the Hester Street market. They were able to indulge their passion for shirt-waists – not fashionable taffeta or silk ones but fine, warm cashmere ones, at a quarter the price they cost in the stores and they bought woollen walking skirts to go with them. Gertrude advised Annie against buying fashionable button boots and persuaded her to invest in a pair of the new rubber overshoes instead, which would serve her better in the harsh conditions out west. A pair of stout boots each, a grey wool cape for Annie and their purchases were complete.

The shopping trip was followed by a visit to Monroe Street, where Gertrude met Annie's family for the first time. Her simple, friendly manner won them over and Annie could see immediately that her parents liked and trusted the older girl. There was an air of excitement as the whole family gathered for a farewell supper that evening at 32 Monroe Street. Even Tom managed to make it along accompanied by Molly, and a little later, to Annie's delight, Sophia arrived on a brief break from the hospital, anxious to bid farewell to her friend.

Mother had baked a special pie for the occasion and

Auntie Norah had brought along some of her famous mince pies which Annie had not tasted in a long time. There was much laughter and gaiety as they all crowded around the table in the Moores' small living-room.

'Faith then, 'tisn't every day one of the family becomes a runner and runs off to Nebraska,' protested Uncle Charlie when Aunt Norah chided him for helping himself to a third slice of Mother's delicious pie. The boys laughed uproariously at this.

'Sure maybe you'll all come out and join me. You've said you might go homesteading one day, Father,' said Annie.

'Wait and see, girl, wait and see,' replied Father, who never liked to commit himself. 'Farming green pastures is one thing but homesteading out west is another story.'

'I think your father was thinking more of somewhere a little nearer,' Mother added tactfully. 'Not so far west. Perhaps Virginia, where it's green and fertile – not unlike the old country.'

'You folk can never forget the "old country", as you call it, can you,' sighed Tom, who now considered himself one hundred per cent American and never gave a thought to his homeland. He greatly admired his sister for her adventurous spirit, and although he wouldn't quite tell her as much, he secretly envied her.

Molly and Annie smiled at one another. They could sense a political argument on the way. Whenever father and son got together sparks would fly, with Uncle Charlie playing referee. Annie was happy. It had been a long time since the family had enjoyed a gathering such as this. She was so grateful not to be leaving them with a cloud hanging over her head. They had finally accepted her version of what had happened at the Van der Leutens' and this was an enormous relief to her. Now, no matter how far she travelled she would always have a loving family to return to. And, looking at Molly and Sophia, she saw true friends she knew she could always count on.

The thought struck her that it would have been just perfect if Mike had come to say goodbye but the instant she had the thought, she knew it was untrue. She didn't need to see Mike just now. It was enough to know that he wished her well and to hope that when they met again in the future it would be under better circumstances. As she felt a lump rising in her throat, she pushed the thought of him away.

She thought back to the day she had sailed from Queenstown, when she had thought her heart would break with the loneliness of leaving Uncle Charlie and Auntie Norah even though she was going to join her parents in America. Yet here they were again, all united in America. Now she was on the brink of another departure but it was different this time. She was older and, she hoped, a lot wiser. She was going to Nebraska of her own volition and she knew she could return to New York whenever she wished. She felt hopeful that this time there was nothing to fear, nothing to lose.

8

ALL ABOARD FOR NEBRASKA!

'All aboard, all aboard for Chicago! This way for sleep-ing-car passengers!' A porter expertly grabbed the girls' baggage, bringing it directly to the sleeping car while Uncle Charlie found them good window seats in the adjacent seating compartment. It was Saturday after-noon and the whole family except Tom, who was on duty at the hotel, had assembled to wave them off. It was just as well the girls had arrived early for as the time of departure approached, a flurry of passengers arrived to board and some found themselves standing as there were no seats left. Suddenly they heard a long shrill whistle and the moment of departure was upon them.

'Goodbye, goodbye. I'll write as soon as I arrive. Take good care of Mother . . . ' Annie's final words were lost in the explosive hiss of steam from the engine as they pulled swiftly away from the platform. Running along-side, Anthony and Philip waved to their sister and her friend until they could no longer be seen.

Within half an hour they had left the city behind and

were pulling out into the darkening landscape. The adventure had only just begun.

What a novelty it was for Annie, who had only ever travelled by train from Macroom to Cork and from Cork to Queenstown, to travel long-distance. Gertrude, a seasoned traveller, took great pleasure in showing her companion the ropes. Annie soon found out why Gertrude had insisted on bringing a hamper of food to get them through until the following morning. There was a dining-car on board to be sure, but it was expensive for dinner, whereas they could enjoy the dining-car equally over breakfast, which was relatively cheap.

'And it will be daylight then so we can admire the view at the same time,' said Gertrude. She also had to warn Annie not to buy anything from the peddlers they saw stalking swiftly through the carriages offering all sorts of items at inflated prices – fruit, candy, buttons, novelties and newspapers. One gentleman sitting nearby had been furious to discover that he had been sold yesterday's newspapers.

'Young whipper-snapper,' he snorted in disgust. 'Him and his tray of Yankee notions!'

The girls were relieved when the gentlemen travelling in their carriage eventually took themselves off to the smoking car and they could eat their impromptu meal without being enveloped by clouds of smoke.

Soon it was time to settle down for the night. Moving into the sleeping car, Annie was reminded of her voyage across the Atlantic a few years previously. Rows of bunks lined the walls of the carriage, but oh how much more civilised it was compared with the steamer. The

Pintsch lighting throughout the train was dim here with tiny little lamps over each bunk and the bedclothes folded back invitingly.

Nonetheless, lying in the narrow bunk that night, she soon realised that the rocking motion of the train was just as disturbing as the rolling of the ship. Many times she thought she'd be pitched right out of the top bunk. Seeing Gertrude sleep peacefully on a lower one, she wished she had chosen more sensibly.

As soon as dawn broke, however, she was up to look out the window. They would make their first stop in Cleveland in less than an hour's time. Although it was quite near one of the great Canadian lakes they would only be able to catch a glimpse of it from the train.

Later as they feasted on coffee and buckwheat griddle cakes in the dining car and were waited on hand and foot, she did indeed enjoy a glorious view of the pleasant, fertile countryside stretching out on either side.

After stopping at Detroit, it would be non-stop to Chicago, and the conductor who inspected their tickets promised them a splendid view of Lake Michigan later on in the day. Annie busied herself without further ado. She had revived her journal – the very one given to her by her Cork friend Julia Donohue before she'd left Ireland. Now she would have time to write in it. There was so much to record already – and she was sure there was so much to come.

'Chicago, thirty-five minutes,' cried the conductor. The evening of the second day had closed in and again Annie found herself peering through the gathering darkness, to see the lights of that famous city welcome them in.

'Tomorrow, we'll awake in Nebraska.' Gertrude's usually calm voice had become tinged with excitement.

After a couple of hours' wait in Chicago – where they slumped wearily on the long wooden benches, surrounded by their baggage – they boarded the Union Pacific's night sleeper bound for Omaha. Annie noticed immediately how different the West-bound passengers seemed from the townsfolk who had travelled from New York to Chicago.

'Cow-hands,' whispered Gertrude, seeing Annie stare openly at a group of men in high leather boots and wide hats who passed through their carriage. They seemed almost too big for the carriage and too loud too. Real outdoors men they looked, so different to city folk.

Though not quite as comfortable as the train from New York, they nonetheless slept well enough, Annie opting for a lower bunk on this occasion. Little did she expect the scene which met her eyes in the morning. Blinking in amazement, she could see nothing but white for miles and miles. They could be on the moon, for all the signs of habitation to be seen.

'Gertrude, wake up,' she urged. 'There's snow everywhere, nothing but snow.'

'Yes, we're in the West now, what else did you expect?' Gertrude yawned sleepily, quite accustomed to the startlingly white landscape spreading on all sides. 'Mind, snow's come early this year,' she added. 'Just in time for Thanksgiving.'

They were due in Omaha by mid-morning and by the

time they had breakfasted and got their belongings together, they heard the conductor announce, 'Omaha, fifteen minutes.'

Rolling closer to the city, the first signs of habitation appeared and Gertrude was soon identifying the different landmarks for her friend. The size of the granaries dotted throughout the landscape was what most amazed Annie.

Omaha did not seem at all similar to New York or Chicago. It looked quite small, with plenty of low, squat buildings and no high-rises. As they drew to a stop in the station, two young men emerged from the crowd and suddenly Gertrude was in the arms of one of them while the other shook Annie's hand heartily and bid her welcome.

This was Gertrude's brother Carl and there was no need for Annie to ask who the other one was.

'My Eric,' Gertrude said simply, turning around with shining eyes to introduce her friend to her fiancé, a tall and well-built young man with typical Swedish looks – blond hair and piercingly blue eyes.

'You are very welcome to Nebraska.' Smiling, he shook Annie's hand vigorously, barely glancing at her. It was clear he had eyes only for Gertrude.

Within minutes they were tucked up in an old farm wagon, surrounded by all their luggage with Carl and Eric perched up on the high front seat. Eric took the reins and guided the horse out on to the frozen streets. Though the sun was shining brightly and the sky a vivid blue, it was bitterly cold and the girls were glad of the big rug to huddle in. Looking around, Annie was stunned that Omaha should be described as a city. Compared to New York, it seemed makeshift and shabby, with buildings that looked more like shacks lining its slush-covered main streets.

Their destination, Douglas County, was not a great distance away. There Gertrude's family all lived close together in a small settlement called Miller's Creek. This was where her grandfather had first staked his claim to a homestead in the seventies and, despite grasshopper plagues, prairie fires and drought, had clung on and survived to be rewarded for his fortitude during the more prosperous eighties. Gertrude had told Annie of the family's early struggles and how they had eventually triumphed over them. Somehow the story had left Annie with the impression that they were still poor struggling immigrants so it was with some surprise that a couple of hours later she awoke from an uneasy slumber, in which she thought her bones would be rattled to breaking point and the rest of her body turned into ice, to behold a fine timber-frame farmhouse surrounded by trees and outbuildings looming up in front of them out of the now foggy and darkening landscape.

Although it was only mid-afternoon, there were lights to be seen in every window and a welcoming lantern on the porch. As they drove up the avenue, the front door was flung open and a number of adults and children surged out and down the steps towards them, all laughing and waving excitedly.

'At last, at last,' they called. 'Welcome home.'

Then they were ushered inside to the cosy, well-lit

living room, warmed by the glowing stove right in the centre of the room.

Within minutes Annie had been introduced to the entire family from Grandfather – a white-haired old man smoking his pipe in a fireside rocker – down to baby Katrine, Gertrude's youngest niece and as new to her as she was to Annie.

Gertrude had spoken so much and so feelingly of her family that Annie felt she was already acquainted with the immediate members of it and had no difficulty remembering her sisters' and brothers' names. Matilde, the eldest, was married to Fred and they were the parents of little Katrine as well as two strapping boys of ten and seven years of age, Hans and Will. Then there was Bertha, who was married to Frank, and their twin babies Marja and Lena, as well as Sara, Gertrude's younger sister, still a schoolgirl. Carl, who was nineteen, she had met at the station and her other brother Ivan was a fifteen-year-old who immediately reminded her of Anthony with his curly red hair and cheeky smile.

Gertrude's Mama and Papa, Johanna and Carl Lindgren, were just as she had described them. Annie could straightaway see that Gertrude had got her plump, jolly looks and matching temperament from her mother, while her father was a tall, spare man, kindly and quiet-spoken.

The talk around the table at supper that evening was all of crop failure and how the drought of the previous season had affected their lives. Gertrude's family, it seemed, had not been as badly affected as some because while her father and brothers now worked the family farm, her sisters had not married into farming families. Bertha's husband Frank had an excellent job with the Burlington Railroad Company and Fred, Matilde's husband, was a senior clerk at the Omaha State Bank. Eric, however, owned the neighbouring farm, where Gertrude was soon to join him. He had suffered losses of crops and livestock and was glad he had not had a young wife to support at that time. Now that Gertrude was back, however, his normal optimism had returned and he felt he could face anything.

It had been a hard two years' separation for both of them; they had only decided to live apart when the droughts had set in a few years previously.

'It's a sure way for us to put money by,' Gertrude had insisted and now indeed their foresightedness was vindicated and his fiancée had returned with a tidy little sum saved, which would greatly help them to set up home together next summer. Although he fully trusted his Gertrude, Eric had secretly feared that if she stayed too long in New York he would lose her to some sophisticated city-slicker who could offer her more than he ever could. But looking at her now he could not understand how he could have suspected such a thing would ever happen. She had the truest of true hearts, his Trudie.

'You'll find things quite bad out west where you're headed,' Gertrude's father informed Annie, who was reminded of her own father's warnings of hardship and drought and all manner of disaster.

'My friends are doing well enough, I think,' she responded hesitantly, reflecting that Ellen's letters had given very little detail of her circumstances.

'Well, all I can say is that we heard stories of how's the folk out there was near starvin' last winter,' he remarked, looking at her doubtfully. 'An' it's bin just as bad this year.'

'Those folk are all in debt to their armpits,' added Fred, nodding knowingly. 'But I guess they ain't goin' to invite you out there if they can't feed you,' he said kindly, with a twinkle in his eye.

'Pa, don't you be putting Annie off now. She's real keen and she'll be a welcome sight to them. Her friend Ellen is expecting her first and she'll be needing the help and the company for sure,' said Gertrude, smiling reassuringly at her friend.

The next few days passed quickly and Annie grew to love Gertrude's family and Miller's Creek, where she got her first taste of life on a farm. Gertrude showed her all the livestock and Carl brought her around the neighbourhood in the farm wagon when he was delivering milk. On these occasions, however, she sat up on the high front bench beside him while Hans and Will rattled around in the wagon box, and once he even let her take the reins on a straight stretch of the trail uphill to Eric's farm, which had been cleared of snow. They chatted as they went and Annie told him about life in the East and how she had just learned to ride a bicycle.

'I'm thinkin' it's a horse you ought to be learnin' to ride now,' Carl remarked drily, adding that if the ground hadn't been snow-covered, he would have gladly taught her.

By the time they all sat down to Thanksgiving dinner a few days later, Annie felt as if she'd been with the

Lindgrens for years, and she was reluctant to pack her bags again the next day and be on her way west again. But when she thought of Ellie, who must now surely be looking forward greatly to her friend's arrival, she felt ashamed and got her bags ready with renewed enthusiasm for the 'great adventure'.

Carl would drive her back to Omaha two days after Thanksgiving and they would be accompanied by Gertrude, who said she would take the opportunity to shop in Omaha, although Annie knew her friend was really coming to give her the best send-off she could. They set off very early in the morning in order to catch the train west at ten o'clock. Despite the early hour, most of the family waved them off and Annie's heart sank a little as she left the kindness and warmth of Gertrude's family behind and set off into the unknown. It was dark when they left, wrapped up as snugly as possible in the wagon. Gertrude, seeing her friend's slightly anxious expression, did her best to reassure her.

'Remember, Annie, that if you are unhappy there for any reason you will always be welcome here. In any case, Eric and I hope you will be able to come to our wedding next summer. You promise me?'

'Of course I do,' Annie replied, wondering where she would be and what she would be doing by next summer.

'Only if you've learned to ride a horse though,' joked Carl from his perch at the front. He had grown quite fond of Annie in the few days she had spent with them and he would miss joking with her.

When the train took off finally and she had waved her friends goodbye, she settled down contentedly to catch up on all the letters she had promised to write to family and friends. That and her journal occupied her so completely that despite an occasional glance at the snow-clad countryside and a break to eat the delicious lunch Mama Lindgren had packed for her, she hardly noticed the day passing until she heard the announcement: 'Kimball, forty-five minutes.'

It seemed only minutes from then until she saw Ellen, the same Ellen she'd left three years ago on Ellis Island, waiting to greet her. And suddenly all her doubts melted away. The tall, dark handsome man who stood beside her was, no doubt, her husband Dan and a fine couple they made, she thought as she jumped delightedly from the train and into Ellen's waiting embrace.

'Let me see you,' cried Ellen, holding her at arm's length. 'My, what a beauty you've grown into. A right New York lady now and no mistake! Isn't she, Dan?'

'You shore are welcome to Kimball, Nebraska, Miss Annie Moore,' said Dan in mock Western tones, bowing low over her hand.

9

—

THE HOUSE ON THE PRAIRIE

Later, when Annie looked back on her arrival in Kimball she realised she had almost no memory of the night spent with one of Ellen's sisters in the town before they set off on the long-haul wagon trip to Scott's Bluff, where Ellen and Dan lived. She put this down to exhaustion. She had travelled so far and met so many new people in one short week. Being naturally proud – Father would say cussed – she was unwilling to admit that it could have been the shock of seeing her new home with the young couple that had blocked out all memory of what had gone before.

It was early evening – just getting dark – when they finally arrived at Scott's Bluff in Dan's small covered wagon. Annie was so cold she could hardly jump down from the wagon without help when they drew up at the little sod-house miles out on the prairie. Looking around at the darkening skies she could see that there was no other house or building of any description within sight – just endless snow-clad prairie, the only sound the howling wind which had blown up in the last couple of hours. While Dan went to unharness the horses, Ellen brought Annie into the little house that seemed to burrow into the low hill behind it for protection from the elements.

Annie had never before heard of a sod-house – or 'soddy' as Ellen affectionately described it. She could hardly believe her eyes when she saw that it was a house made of sods of earth dug out of the ground. The roof even had clumps of rough scutch grass growing out of it and a crude stove-pipe stuck out the top in place of a chimney. She was reassured at least to see two timber-framed windows and a solid wooden door.

'You'll see, Annie, it will be really warm when we get the fire going,' said Ellen, seeing her friend's dazed expression as they entered what seemed to Annie like a cold, dark shed with only a dirt floor. When the lamps were lit and the stove going, Annie glimpsed the interior, which, though plain and stark, looked homely enough. There appeared to be only two rooms, the living-room they were standing in and the bedroom. Where would she sleep, she wondered, feeling that at any moment she would burst into tears. How was she going to live in a godforsaken place like this? Why had Ellie not warned her what it would be like?

Sensing her predicament, Ellen put her arm around Annie's shoulders and hugged her. 'You must be worn out with the travel and all,' she said gently. 'Let me show you where you're to sleep; it isn't so bad,' and she drew Annie to the corner at the back of the room where a small rectangle partitioned off from the living-room contained a neatly made-up truckle bed and a bedside chair.

The best thing in the soddy was the stove, Annie decided straightaway – a grand Franklin stove which stood plumb in the middle of the living-room floor with its stove-pipe leading straight up through the roof – this was the 'chimney' she'd seen from outside. It threw out great heat, she soon discovered, and by the time she'd tidied her trunk away under the bed and hung up some clothes on the hooks across the partition, it already had the place warmed up and Ellen was cooking supper on it. Dan had come in and within minutes the three were sitting down to a meal of cornmeal pancakes with chokeberry jelly, washed down with good strong, hot coffee.

The next morning dawned clear and sunny and, though still fiercely cold, the wind had died down and Annie, having slept off most of her exhaustion, felt a good deal more cheerful. The farm consisted of 160 acres mostly set in corn, two milking cows, a sow and some hens. While Dan was off repairing fences that morning, the girls had their first chance to have a good long chat, Ellen working as they talked and Annie, wrapped up in the warmest garments she could find, trying her best to help. The house looked more attractive in daylight with pots of red geraniums ranged along the wooden frame window-sill and, to her surprise, still flowering in the cold of November.

Annie was reassured by their talk and though she was still in for a few shocks about their homesteading lifestyle, she was encouraged enough by the end of that first day to feel she just might be able to make a go of it.

'You know, it seems harder than it is, truly, Annie,' Ellen remarked, well aware that her friend was still shocked at how and where they lived. 'When I came here first I felt I couldn't live here like this. Mind, I stayed with my sister Kathleen then and at the time, God knows, they had three small children as well as myself living in this little house. But it was only six months before I moved into Kimball to work. Not long after that Kathleen and John built a frame-house over in Wildcat Ridge. By that time, Dan and I were planning to marry and they offered us the property at a good price. So here we are. They only live about eight miles north of here. You'll meet them all soon.'

She then related how she had found work as a teacher in Kimball. There she had lived with her other sister Maisie who, with her husband Ted, ran a boarding house. It was here she had met Dan McAllister, a young prospector only a couple of years left Ireland – a Corkman – who had been on his way to Oregon to dig for gold when he met Ellen.

'It was love at first sight, he says,' Ellen laughed. 'But it took me some time to see it. I think I was of half a mind to return home to Ireland at that time. But he changed my mind. I'm glad he did,' she said with feeling. Dan's plans to prospect for gold were abandoned and he decided it was time to settle down.

Annie looked at her with wonder. While she could see how happy she and Dan were together, she couldn't imagine that Ellie would want to live like this for the rest of her days.

As if reading her thoughts, Ellen said, 'You know we don't plan to bring up our family in this house, Annie. Dan already has plans drawn up for building our own frame-house here. He hopes to start in spring. He's planted trees as a shelter belt over there already, you see.' Right enough Annie could see the weather-beaten little saplings sticking out of the snow over the far side of the lean-to. 'It should be ready for next winter, please God.'

Annie was to learn a lot of tough lessons about homesteading over the next day or so. She was to discover to her horror that the huge pile of dried-out cow pats piled up against the wall of the shed were what Ellen used for fuel.

'Chips' they were called. Old buffalo chips were even better, apparently, but the buffalo had left the area even before the Indians and while the chips could last indefinitely, they were difficult to come by nowadays. There being few trees on that part of the prairie, wood was extremely rare. In autumn after the harvest, Ellen ex-plained, they burned hay and corncobs or sometimes Kathleen and John brought them a load of timber from their generously wooded area, and that would last them for a while.

But worst of all – and something she thought she might never be able to get used to – were the garter snakes, which, though rare enough, were also part and parcel of life in a soddy.

'But they aren't dangerous, Annie,' Ellen explained laughingly the first time Annie encountered one on the kitchen floor and jumped screaming on to the settle.

'Now if it was a rattlesnake you'd be in real trouble. Luckily there aren't too many of them around.'

The real hazards of life out on the prairie were not to be found within the confines of the home but outside it where, Annie learned, blizzards, prairie fires, drought and hot winds could pose a very real threat to the lives of both humans and livestock as well as to the crops. Often at night when Annie lay snug in her bed and the only sound to be heard was the howling of coyotes across the stillness of the plains she realised that there was no one else around them for miles in this bare, white world and she felt like one of the early pioneers.

It was soon established that Annie would pay her way by helping out on the little farm and taking over a number of Ellen's tasks as her time drew near. The baby was expected at the beginning of February. After that, Annie was to feel free to do whatever she chose.

She could perhaps find work in Kimball – Ellen said they were always looking for new teachers in the school there, especially to teach English to the many immigrant children of European families who were still moving into the area – or she could stay on with them at the farm, where she would be more than welcome.

'I'll teach you all I know and you will come to love the place as I have. I know it,' Ellen assured her.

In the weeks running up to Christmas, Annie learned a tremendous amount. As she wrote Molly in New York:

I've learned to do things that I never thought I could. I'm milking the two cows now and feeding and collecting the eggs from the hens as well as cleaning out the hen house. All the animals have got to know me now and I'm even learning to horse-ride. But you'll be shocked to hear that none of the women ride side-saddle out here but astride. Ellie had to give me her divided skirts to be comfortable. She can't wear them or ride the horses now because of her condition but she promises we'll go riding together in spring. Mind, the horses are right old nags, really only good for pulling the plough and drawing the wagon and they never go very fast, but they do fine for someone like me.

You cannot imagine how different life on the prairie is to life in New York. Though I have had doubts lots of times and wondered why I gave up a comfortable life in the city, I am beginning to think that it was the right thing for me to do. I am learning to do things that I never would do in the city and the people I've met – like Ellie's sisters and their families – are so straight and also kind. I've rarely met their like.

They were to spend Christmas at Kathleen and John's home in Wildcat Ridge only eight miles away and Annie was looking forward to it. Their timber-frame house set at the edge of an evergreen forest with breathtaking views of the surrounding countryside seemed like a palace to her in her present circumstances. Trees were an unusual enough sight on the plains of Nebraska and she had been astounded at the sight of the tree-covered hills of this area, so different to the flat prairie land she inhabited with Ellen and Dan.

One trip to Kimball to buy provisions for the season was planned for the week before Christmas. They would rise extra early to feed the livestock and Ned Cady, their nearest neighbour a couple of miles east, would drop by to see to them, which would allow them to stay overnight with Maisie and Ted. Setting off on the clear December morning, they saw the sun rise over the prairies as they drove along the trail bordering the bluff and Annie marvelled at the sight. All around her there seemed to be only sky, with streaks of pink softening the harsh glare of the snow-covered plains. The silence was as immense as the sky and as they trotted along, the only sound to be heard was the horses' hooves churning up the snow, tempered with the occasional whinny as they encountered a difficult patch where the snow was deeper and the ground more uneven.

Perhaps it was because she was now more adjusted to her new life or perhaps it was just sheer good spirits but Annie felt a sense of elation just to be alive. Having hardly taken in the sight of Kimball on the night of her arrival, she was excited to be returning to meet Maisie and Ted and their family again and to be able to do a little Christmas shopping as well as mail off her letters to New York.

While Dan tied up the team outside the lumber yard, where he had business to do, Ellen and Annie had a wonderful time shopping in the low-slung wooden build-ings along the boardwalks on Main Street, where there was a drugstore, a general store and a bank. The post office and the railway station were at the other end of town beside the lumber yard. Horses tied up at the hitch-bars along the frozen street stamped impatiently from time to time and swished their tails, knowing well that their owners were savouring the warmth and excitement inside the stores, sheltered from the harsh relentless wind, and would be in no hurry to rescue them.

Everywhere they went Ellen introduced Annie and people nodded in a friendly way and wished her good luck. There was a good crowd of people about, all the country people like themselves in town to do their Christmas shopping. They looked after the provisions first and stored them in the wagon and then off they went in search of Christmas gifts.

The evening was spent with Maisie and Ted and their two daughters, Emma and Laura, making plans for Christ-mas over a grand hot supper of spare ribs and 'taters', as they called potatoes. It was fun. Laura was Annie's own age and the two hit it off immediately. All three girls stayed awake for hours, Annie telling them about her voyage to America with their Aunt Ellen as well as all about life in New York City. They couldn't hear enough and before they finally fell into an exhausted sleep Annie had promised them both that they could travel back east with her whenever she was going.

It was back to hard work the next day and they only reached home in the nick of time before a blizzard set in and for the next few days they seemed as good as buried in their little soddy. Dan could barely struggle as far as the lean-to to feed the cattle and from there to the hen-house. You couldn't see a yard in front of your nose and as soon as you made tracks in any direction the snow covered them over. When Dan told Annie of how people had been buried in snow in their own front yard she could well believe it.

Thankfully, however, it all lifted before Christmas Eve and they were able to set off early on Christmas morning for Wildcat Ridge in bright sunshine and very little wind. The weather had called a seasonal truce. Dan was to return alone early the following morning and the girls would be driven home a couple of days later by Maisie and Ted on their way back to Kimball.

It was a memorable Christmas. Annie had thought that she would be lonesome without her own family but she had hardly a minute to think about them.

By the time all twelve sat down to dinner, the light was fading outside. The younger children, who had been playing in the snow and trying out the new sled John had built them, came in as hungry as young coyotes. Maisie's two girls, as well as Annie, had been pressed into service to arrange the table in a suitably festive way. Already the cosy wooden house was decorated with twigs of the heavily scented pine trees which grew all around while the Christmas tree they'd placed in the big window overlooking the valley was festooned with pine cones painted all colours of the rainbow, popcorn balls, strings of cranberries and little parcels of candy.

Underneath the tree was a growing bundle of presents of all sizes and shapes. When the moment finally came to open them, cries of delight echoed all around and Annie was amazed at the ingenuity of some of the homely presents the families exchanged – home-made candles and bars of soap in unlikely shapes as well as hand-knit mittens and mufflers. Not only had John built his children a sled but he now presented his wife with a rocking-chair he had also fashioned himself.

Christmas dinner was a feast indeed – roasted chickens with gravy and sweet potatoes and pumpkin pie followed by preserves and wild fruit.

After the meal, they all gathered around the big stove in the candlelight and sang songs – Annie had them all spellbound with her rendering of 'Oft in the Stilly Night'.

'What a beautiful voice the girl has,' said Kathleen admiringly.

'Didn't I tell you now,' said Ellen proudly.

Indeed Annie wasn't the only one able to sing and by midnight they had all contributed. Many an Irish song was sung, making Annie a little nostalgic for her family in New York and indeed for the old country, which she'd noticed had been rapidly receding from her memory in recent times. But even better was to come.

Their host, Ellen's brother-in-law John, she was to learn, was a marvellous storyteller – they called him the 'seanchaí' of the family, although the stories he had to tell had nothing to do with Ireland but with the country of his adoption. That night Annie heard accounts of prairie fires and Indian raids that made her hair stand on end. But it was the one about the grasshopper plague of the '70s that really riveted them all.

'Back in the 1870s newcomers to Nebraska had worse problems to deal with than you'd find in these parts nowadays,' John began, stoking the fire with a poker and sitting down again. Everyone fell silent expectantly.

'It was on a beautiful hot day in July of '74 that it all started,' he began in his deep, low voice. 'Suddenly a dark cloud blocked out the sun and then a roaring noise like a gathering storm was heard. People looked up from their work and within minutes they found themselves almost in darkness as this huge cloud descended over them and they saw, to their horror, that it wasn't a cloud at all, only millions and millions of large grasshoppers landing on top of them. As big as locusts, they were. Wherever they landed they covered the earth thickly like a crawling carpet. Then they began to eat everything in sight, the crops, the leaves on the trees, the vegetables, the flowers, everything. Even clothing was reduced to shreds. In one day everything was destroyed.'

John paused and looked around him. His audience was intent, not an eye flickered or looked away. He continued. 'The animals feasted on them but that was not enough to get rid of them. They drove the horses wild by flying into their faces. They got into the barns and ate their way through the grain which had been stored for the winter. They even invaded people's homes if they had no screen doors and ate all their food, and gnawed at their furniture. But the very worst thing about them was that they laid hundreds of eggs so when the first ones died off there were more to take their place. The farmers were ruined. There had been a drought that year anyway and crops were bad. But this finished them off and many had to leave their farms and return east.

'It was a common sight then to see a poor, discouraged family pack up and leave. And scrawled on the covers of their wagons would be the words: 'Eaten out by grasshoppers. Going back east.'

John stopped and looked around him. By this time, the little ones were looking terrified and Kathleen jumped up and lit the lamps and even Annie was relieved to hear that grasshopper plagues were a thing of the past and that they had disappeared as mysteriously as they had come and hadn't been seen in these parts for about twenty years.

Dan returned home the following morning, leaving the two girls to enjoy the festivities at Wildcat Ridge, promising to have everything ready for their return to Scott's Bluff a couple of days later. But nothing prepared them for the surprise that was in store for them when they alighted from Maisie and Ted's wagon and re-entered their humble soddy. Dan stood proudly awaiting their cries of delight when they stepped onto a gleaming, new wooden floor. He had ordered the wood on their trip to Kimball before Christmas and had had it delivered to Ned Cady and stored at his place. Indeed he couldn't have managed without Ned, who had come over and helped him lay the new floor in the past couple of days.

'We'll have to have a dance to christen it,' cried Ellen, throwing her arms around his neck in gratitude and delight. 'That's the best Christmas present, love.'

'No, Ellie,' laughed Dan, 'more like we'll christen first and dance after.'

10

Enter James Scott McAllister

As the weeks went by and Ellen's time drew near, she had to hand over many of her outdoor tasks to Annie. Growing in confidence every day, Annie felt she could tackle anything. The cold, dry air of Nebraska suited her and she had not been ill one single day since her arrival. In New York she would surely have had a couple of attacks of bronchitis by now.

She had become so confident on horseback that she had even taken old Bess and ridden over to Wildcat Ridge occasionally on an errand, starting off very early and riding back before darkness fell. She joked to Ellen and Dan that if she had not known the way to get there herself, Bess would have brought her there and back directly anyway, so well did the old horse know it by now.

So it was that Dan felt he could safely leave them both when word came one morning that Ned Cady's roof was leaking so badly he just couldn't risk waiting until spring to do a major repair job on it. It would have to be done now. Dan knew that if perchance Ellen were to go into labour, Annie would be well capable of fetching him. He could then ride post-haste for the doctor, who lived on the other side of Scott's Bluff, not a great distance from Kimball. But neither Dan nor the girls could have predicted the strength of the blizzard that blew up as soon as he had arrived over at Ned's place. All hope of working on the roof was abandoned and the men waited anxiously for some sign of abatement, Dan keenly aware that Ellen could start having the baby at any time. Inwardly, he cursed himself for having left home at all that day. All he could do now was hope and pray that nothing would happen until this storm blew over.

The two girls at home also watched the onset of the blizzard a little anxiously, knowing it would delay Dan's return. But not wanting to worry each other, neither mentioned their concerns and Ellen continued to work on the tiny quilt she was making for the baby's crib while Annie prepared a stew.

When Ellen felt the first stab of pain, she said nothing, hoping it wasn't serious. But when her waters broke a couple of hours later, neither of them could ignore it and they looked at each other in dismay.

'Don't fret, Ellie,' Annie said as she saw her friend's eyes widen with fright. 'I'll ride over to Ned's and let Dan know right away.' But her voice trailed off as she took a look out the window and saw how, even in the half-hour since she'd last glanced out, the blizzard had worsened. Not a thing was to be seen but the heavily falling snow. It even blocked out sight of the lean-to and although it was only three o'clock in the afternoon, it had become quite dark.

'No, Annie, 'twould be madness to go. The track to Ned's would be well covered by now and you'd be lost. No, you'll have to stay until it stops.' Her voice was tight with panic and Annie decided the best thing to do would be to give all her attention to keeping her friend calm. To get lost in the blizzard would be no help and she'd certainly perish in this cold. She hoped likewise that Dan had the good sense to stay where he was, although she knew he'd be worried. My, if he only knew that his child had decided to ignore all weather warnings and come anyway, she thought to herself.

'Now, Ellie, let's get you comfortable,' she said, sounding more confident than she felt, as she got Ellen into bed. 'You're certainly not going anywhere today,' she joked weakly. Just then Ellen winced as another pain – stronger this time – let her know that this baby was definitely on its way. Inwardly Annie felt panic as she had never even seen a baby being born, let alone helped to deliver one. Her mind raced as she tried to recall what she knew about such an eventuality. She recalled hearing something about keeping everything clean and having lots of hot water at the ready. Oh, but she knew there was lots more to it than that. What would she do at all? If only the doctor were here or even Kathleen or Maisie, who'd been through it all themselves. Please God let Dan come or . . . or anyone, she prayed.

By teatime the pains were coming every five minutes or so and Annie knew it couldn't be long until the baby was born. There was still no sign of any passing of the storm – nor of Dan. She now realised it was all up to her.

Up to now she had helped by rubbing her friend's back and mopping her brow with a damp cloth to comfort her but now she knew that the next stage was fast upon them. The baby was coming and Ellen's breathing was becoming more laboured by the minute. Annie prayed the birth would be normal, as Mother had always told her that unless there was something seriously amiss, a baby's birth was the most natural thing in the world. Before too long, baby James Scott McAllister had arrived, defying the wishes of his mother Ellen and his godmother Annie. Thankfully, he made his own way into the world with only the minimum of help from them both.

Nor did he lose any time in letting them know that he was tired and hungry after his journey. As the yells of the newborn infant filled the little house, Ellen and Annie laughed and cried together at the sight of him, and Annie, following Ellen's instructions, cut the cord and lifted the precious bundle into his mother's arms.

Later that night – when the storm had finally died down just enough for him to make it home – Dan stepped through his door to the amazing sight of his smiling wife propped against the pillows with her son at her breast and a poor, exhausted Annie slumped heavily in a chair beside the bed fast asleep.

There was great rejoicing over the next few days as word spread about baby Scott's dramatic entrance to the world on the night of the blizzard. Aunts, uncles and cousins gathered from both Wildcat Ridge and Kimball to celebrate his arrival and the grand new wooden floor in the soddy was well and truly christened.

*

At the end of March, when the thaw had set in and the first hint of spring was making itself felt on the prairie, Annie received a message from Ellen's sister Maisie in Kimball to say that an opening was coming up for an assistant to the teacher in the school there.

'I took upon myself the liberty of mentioning your name,' she wrote, 'as I think you could be very good at it. The pay is not high but you might enjoy it and it would give you a chance to meet people here and get to know them. You would be most welcome to board here with us if you are willing to share a room with Laura.'

Annie was indeed interested and straightaway discussed it with Ellen and Dan. Baby Scott was doing very well and Ellen was back on her feet by now and enjoyed bringing her son everywhere with her, tied papoose-like to her back.

'I think it would be good for you,' Ellen remarked. 'It cannot surely do any harm to try it out. You've been such a help to me and Dan but you can't stay here for the rest of your days and besides it will give me all the more excuse to pay visits to town.'

Dan agreed, adding laughingly that he didn't know how much she knew about reading, writing and arithmetic but she could sure teach the skills of homesteading to those townie children now that she'd finished her apprenticeship with them.

The end of that week saw Annie packed up and on

the move once more. It was arranged that John, who was travelling to town to stock up on provisions, would take Annie along with him. Dan and a now stronger-looking Ellen, holding baby Scott in her arms, waved them off.

'Take care of my godson,' called Annie, waving until her friends had become mere dots on the prairie land-scape.

The drive to Kimball, on a mild, bright March day, was as different from their last trip there, in mid-winter, as it possibly could be and Annie felt a surge of excitement at the prospect of another imminent adventure. She smiled as she thought of Molly's sur-prise when she heard that her friend was going to try her hand at teaching. She must be sure to write and tell her soon and ask for some advice and counsel on the subject.

She thought back to Molly's latest missive, which was full of news of New York and all the latest doings of the Women's Suffrage League. She assured Annie that there was sure to be a branch of that organisation in Kimball – 'or Lincoln at least,' she wrote, 'and you could be our representative in the West.' Molly obviously had no idea how far apart Lincoln and Kimball were, Annie thought.

Molly herself was now a fully qualified kindergarten teacher in Brooklyn and loved it. 'It is all I've ever wanted to do', she wrote. Although she mentioned Tom often in her letters – the two were still walking out – she never once mentioned Mike. Annie pondered on whether this was good or bad. If Mike had become betrothed to Clara, Molly would be sure to have mentioned it, she reassured herself. Bother! Although she had persuaded herself many times that she had as good as forgotten Mike, she nonetheless found her thoughts straying back to him from time to time. She resolved to put all such thoughts from her mind and tried to concentrate on the adventure ahead.

Though quite an ordinary boarding house, Maisie and Ted's house seemed like a spacious Newport mansion to Annie after being so closely confined in the soddy for the past four months, and she found sharing the big attic bedroom with Laura no hardship whatsoever. Laura was apprentice to a seamstress but was hoping to go into business on her own as a milliner eventually, and the two girls had to share the room with many hats in different stages of production.

'I hope you won't mind, Annie,' said Laura apologetically, 'but I need to be working on them and I've no space elsewhere.'

'As long as you let me try them out whenever I wish,' retorted Annie, smiling.

'What a fine idea. You could be my model when I sell them,' cried Laura, her eyes shining. She could see already how Annie's magnificent mane of auburn hair could enhance her hats in potential customers' eyes. Within minutes the girls were planning their strategy and by that first teatime Laura's millinery business had been nearly dreamed into reality. By Monday morning, when Annie was to report to the school, she had settled into Maisie and Ted's like a member of the family.

Although it was the first week in April, the weather

had suddenly turned nasty again and strong gales swept through the little town. Annie felt she would be blown right out of Main Street as she struggled down to the school early on Monday morning. It was one of the last buildings on the street near the lumber yard.

She was to meet the schoolmistress before classes began. Miss Matilda Hammond was a rather genteel lady not long arrived from Boston. A widow, she boarded in a room above the cobbler's nearby. Her grey hair, tied back in a tight bun at the nape of her neck, and her bespectacled face gave her a very severe appearance. However, she was welcoming to her new recruit.

'I am pleased to see you, Miss Moore,' she said. 'My assistant has been taken ill and she won't be back for some time. I hope you will be able to stay with us until the summer vacation. You will look after the younger children. I look after the older ones. Let me show you the schoolroom.'

To Annie's surprise, the school consisted of only one large schoolroom, heated by a large stove with a makeshift screen of cane straddling the centre. It was sparsely furnished with benches, and she saw that wooden crates doubled for desks and the benches were only planks of wood propped up by boulders or other smaller boxes. A simple chair and table for each teacher and a blackboard completed the school's equipment. Annie would be responsible for fifteen of the school's twenty-five children and these would range in age from five to twelve years of age.

'The pay is low enough – $65 a month plus $10 board,' explained Miss Hammond, to Annie's further amazement – she hadn't thought to be paid such a grand wage – 'and we haven't got many books here so anything you can contribute will be most welcome. As it is we have some Webster's blue-back spellers and enough McGuffey's readers to go around. We're short of Smith and Smiley's arithmetic right now but we can share them around until I get some more sent from Lincoln. We're not too badly off for dictionaries and almanacs but bring in anything you have; it will sure come in handy.'

Annie wondered if the same books were used to teach all age-groups. She got no chance to ask, however, as the children began filing into the schoolroom. Within minutes she was surrounded – an immediate object of curiosity to the town's schoolchildren.

Who was she? Where had she come from? How long would she stay? It seemed the children had a million questions to ask and it took the best part of the morning before she and Miss Hammond had them settled to their usual tasks.

By the end of that first school day, Annie was exhausted and her voice hoarse from trying to make herself heard above the din in the schoolroom, and she was inclined to think that work out on the farm was a darn sight more easygoing. However, she had instantly developed a rapport with the children in her charge, finding them bright and lively as well as curious. She could see that she was going to have to organise her day's work in advance and have plenty prepared for each of the age-groups within her group to keep them going if she wanted to be in control.

'But it's fun. I think I'm going to like it,' she told Maisie when she arrived home that afternoon. She wasted no time before writing off to Molly for advice, also asking for any cast-off books she might have, knowing how much better-equipped the schools back east would be.

As the weeks went by and the weather became warmer the sheer beauty of this wild grassy landscape became evident to Annie. On Sundays, she and Laura often saddled the two horses and rode out of the small town on to the prairie, only a few minutes distant. They would ride to where the sky seemed to be all around them and the earth looked like a sea of waving yellow corn.

Here Annie would stop momentarily and gaze out towards Scott's Bluff wondering how Ellen and Dan and baby Scott were faring. Despite her busy life she missed them and longed to see them again. Indeed it was planned she would go and help them out during the threshing season, which would coincide with her summer vacation from school. In the meantime, Ellen was due to come to town soon for a visit with the baby and she looked forward to it.

She thought too of her family in New York, who now seemed so far away. While letters were frequently exchanged and all of her family appeared fascinated with Annie's accounts of life in the West, it was not quite the same as being able to see them.

'You would love it here, I know,' Annie wrote, 'besides the air would be so good for little Pat and he'd grow up healthy and strong. Anthony and Philip could learn to ride and rustle cattle or some such and you and father might start a boarding house like Maisie and Ted's or even farm, though, God knows, farming is a lot harder than I guessed and there are plenty of opportunities in the town. Uncle Charlie might set up a store with Auntie Norah's help. I am not being fanciful. After all, you are mighty surprised at me becoming a school teacher, now isn't that so?'

Meanwhile, Molly had come to her aid again, sending a large parcel of schoolbooks that she had discarded and writing an encouraging letter about the school-teaching.

'I am so happy that you appear to be enjoying it, as indeed I do myself. I would strongly advise you, however, to think of getting some training as you will soon require a proper certificate to continue as an assistant teacher, even out west.

'There are teaching institutes in many towns and I know there's one in Lincoln. There they would let you work while being trained at the same time so you would not be out of pocket.'

Annie smiled at Molly's presumption that she could attend a training school in Lincoln as if it were close by. However, she knew better than to ignore Molly's advice and maybe if she travelled to Omaha for Gertrude and Eric's marriage in July she might make some enquiries and see if such a thing were possible. In schoolteaching, she, like Molly, had found work she loved and wished to continue with it.

'Let's turn back, Annie. Look at those clouds. I think rain may be on the way.' Laura, her arms full of wild flowers she had been picking, broke into Annie's thoughts and brought her back to earth again.

11

A WEDDING AT MILLER'S CREEK

'Hurray, hurray, school's out, we're free!' the children cried as they ran at full speed out of the schoolroom for the last time until classes resumed in the fall. Privately, Annie echoed the sentiments in her own heart as she packed up her books and prepared to do a last clean-up of the schoolroom. Miss Hammond had left already and Annie was grateful for a few moments to reflect on her first semester of teaching. Yes, she was tired and looking forward to the summer vacation – she had made plans to see Ellen, Dan and her godson and to travel to Miller's Creek for Gertude's wedding – but she had found the work rewarding.

Take Fredrika Olsen, the little Norwegian girl who had not a word of English – nor of any language, so timid was she, Annie first thought – and who was now running around as carefree as the other children, with greatly improved English. Annie had stayed back many an afternoon to give this little girl extra help and it had really paid off. She reminded Annie of Amy, with her blonde braids and big blue eyes.

Then there was Tommy Petersen, who didn't seem to be making any progress, nor did he appear to be even interested in anything until she discovered that in fact he was a little deaf, and she had his parents take him to the doctor. She did extra work with him too, fearful that he would fall behind. Yes, it was a hundred times more rewarding than working as a servant girl, which she would never have to do again, she hoped. Perhaps Molly was right and she should seek some extra training. Well, she would think about it. Now it was time to pack her bags and prepare to spend some time with Ellie and Dan and that little godson of hers in Scott's Bluff. They were in town on a brief visit and she had been overjoyed to see them, unable to believe how Scott had grown in four months. Tomorrow she would travel back with them.

Annie couldn't help but contrast their drive out to Scott's Bluff on this occasion with the misery of her first trip there last November in the relentless cold of mid-winter. Now the plains were transformed into a sea of rippling rust-red grass with masses of huge sun-flowers waving their glorious gold heads on either side of the trail as if to give them a special welcome. The sun shone fiercely out of a blue sky and they were glad of their wide-brimmed hats.

Little Scott slept soundly under cover for most of the journey and only really woke up when they stopped at a creek to eat under the shade of a few puny scrub trees. To Annie's delight most of the sod-houses they passed had flowers growing on the roof, which gave them a wonderfully festive appearance, so unlike the pathetic, cowering sight they'd made in winter.

When they finally arrived the evening was beginning to cool slightly after a sunset so magnificent that they had travelled the last few miles in awed silence. Annie exclaimed aloud in surprise as they drew near the homestead and saw rising up to the right of the soddy a splendid new frame-house with only a roof needed to complete it. She had heard how Dan was working on it but had not realised how far advanced it was.

'It should be completed by the time the harvest is in,' announced Ellen proudly, 'and we'll have moved in by October.'

The next couple of weeks spent with her friends in Scott's Bluff were some of the happiest Annie had spent in a long time. Waking every morning to glorious sunshine, she worked all hours of the day on the farm with Ellen while Dan cut wheat and stacked it with the help of two of Ned Cady's boys and another couple of local hands. It was the busiest time of year for farmers and they worked from dawn to dusk to harvest their crops. But they were more hopeful than they had been for a long time as, thanks to plenty of spring rains this year, there were bumper crops and the threat of drought had lifted for the first time in a few years.

There had also been state aid for those who suffered losses over the past few years, thanks to the hard work of the now-famous Nebraskan Democrat William Jennings Bryan. When Annie heard all about this from Ellen and Dan she wondered wryly if Mike knew about the problems of the farmers in far-off Nebraska or even if he cared one jot about them.

The advantage of the little sod-house was that it was as cool in summer as it had been warm in winter and now sheltered them from the flat heat when it became too much. They did much of their cooking out of doors on a temporary stove rigged up for them by Dan because using the stove inside the soddy would have made it unbearably warm. Ellen even brought out her new sewing machine – a source of pride and joy purchased from the Sears Roebuck catalogue – to continue work on the comforters and drapes for the new house. The two girls spent many happy moments in the evenings when their work was done walking around the new home planning and scheming how it could be fitted out to be worthy of the Mc Allister family.

There were three fine bedrooms, 'so we'll have space for a big family of boys and girls,' said Ellen, holding baby Scott close, and the girls smiled at each other, remembering the shared adventure of his birth.

'Well you had better warn them all to have manners and only come when they're called, not like this little bub,' joked Annie, tickling Scott's toes.

*

It seemed no time at all until Annie was on the move again, back to the other side of Nebraska for Gertrude and Eric's wedding. She looked forward to the adventure now that she had saved enough money for the trip there and back, although she found her thoughts straying frequently to the possibility of staying on to do teacher-training in Lincoln during the next year. She would look into it at least. It could well be that the assistant teacher, whose place she had taken in Kimball, would have recovered and would want her job back by the time the summer vacation was over.

She had discussed Molly's advice with Ellen, who thought teacher-training was an excellent idea and should be seriously considered if Annie felt she could afford it. 'You might not always be living out in the West, Annie,' she said. 'If you returned east you would certainly need a certificate to teach many more subjects than you do in Kimball's little prairie schoolhouse.'

First, however, there was the marriage to think about and Annie was greatly looking forward to visiting Miller's Creek again. When she drew up at the station at Omaha Gertrude and Eric were waiting to meet her.

'Welcome back, dearest Annie,' cried Gertrude, embracing her friend warmly, while Eric's broad grin showed how pleased he was to see his fiancée's friend return. Annie could not but see how happy her friend seemed and recalled the great change in both their lives since they had left the employment of the Van der Leutens.

All the way to Miller's Creek in the wagon the girls exchanged news and Gertrude told of all the preparations for the wedding. They were to be married at home in the Lindgrens' garden by the local Swedish pastor. There would be a feast afterwards of special Swedish dishes and a barn dance to follow.

'I hope you can dance, Annie,' teased Gertrude, knowing her friend loved to dance and would be among the liveliest of all the girls there. 'Carl said he looks forward to showing you how to do the square dance.'

'How does he know I can't do it already,' said Annie, finding herself looking forward to the festivities with increased enthusiasm.

She was received with open arms by the Lindgren family. It was quite late before they were gathered around the table as the threshing had started and the men had all been working until there was almost no light left to see by. As they tucked into their supper with relish the talk again was of the crops and the improvement in this year's harvest. Annie now knew that was what farmers discussed at table all year round.

Here again the name William Jennings Bryan was on everyone's lips and praise for him was unstinting. Of course, being a Lincoln man he was bound to be a hero in these parts, she thought. She was pleased that this time she knew what they were talking about and could tell them how she had heard all about him in west Nebraska. She then found herself telling them about her experiences in Scott's Bluff and Kimball during the past year.

'That Miss Annie has sure become a real Nebraskan sod-buster,' she heard Gertrude's grandpa say with wonder.

'And a schoolmistress too, Grandpa,' added Gertrude.

It was largely left to the women of the Lindgren household to carry out all the preparations for the big day as all of the men and boys, even the eager bridegroom, were entirely taken up with harvesting from morning to night. Naturally, Annie too was pressed into service and helped Gertrude put the finishing touches to the white organza wedding dress and the veil of white tulle which she had made for herself in the past few months. How Laura would love to have been here to oversee this particular task. As they worked, Annie confided her idea of staying on in Lincoln to Gertrude.

'How fine that would be, Annie. You could come and see us more often – it's no great distance.'

'But perhaps they won't take me, Gertrude. I've had very little training, yet I know I can learn.'

'Aunt Marthe might be able to help,' said Gertrude. 'She lives in Lincoln and knows all about these things. I'll make sure you get to meet her when she comes for the wedding.'

The great day dawned warm and windless. The ceremony would take place in the parlour at two o'clock with just family present. Annie was privileged to be the only outsider. A large number of friends and neighbours would arrive later for the wedding feast, which right now was being set up on long tables outside in the garden.

From her window Annie could already see the great barrels of freshly made lemonade being put in place outside the barn where the dance would take place later on. She was looking forward to it all and planned to wear her blue and white muslin dress, which Laura had helped her make for this special occasion. She also planned to wear her hair down – her 'crowning glory', as Uncle Charlie called it. Dear Uncle Charlie, how she missed him sometimes. However, there was no time for dreaming. She should be downstairs by now seeing what she could do to help. But a calm atmosphere prevailed in the house. Johanna Lindgren had already married off two daughters and was well accustomed to such an event. It was only in Gertrude's room that any excitement manifested itself. Matilde and Bertha had arrived and, with Sara, were helping their sister get dressed. Matilde was attaching a headdress of fresh flowers to the veil.

'How beautiful you look, Trudie,' she said, standing back to admire her handiwork. 'Eric is a lucky young man.' With her blonde hair coiled into an intricate topknot Gertrude looked nearly a foot taller than usual. The dress fitted her perfectly and hardly needed the tucking and pinning Bertha was busy giving it.

Finally it was time. Everyone was assembled. Sara would play a wedding march on the family's little parlour organ and Gertrude would walk downstairs on her father's arm.

'We are gathered here today in the sight of the Lord,' the pastor began. Annie's thoughts wandered. The look of great love and trust in Eric's eyes as he turned to greet his young bride had made her eyes fill up. What great love these two shared. Unbidden, her thoughts strayed to Mike. How she had hoped they too would one day come to this stage. But it was not to be, it seemed. Should she ever have left New York, she wondered. But while working in the Van der Leutens' she had never been free to see him anyway. She allowed herself to daydream about what might have been if she had continued to work for him after the fire had closed down the Phoenix Laundry. Suddenly she shook herself. By now she supposed he was Clara's and there was no help for it. She had not had the courage to mention him in her letters back home and had heard nothing about him for a long, long while.

Suddenly it was all over. Gertrude and Eric were man and wife. Sara struck up some joyful music on the organ, the doors were flung open and the party moved out into the garden, where knots of people were already gathering under the shade of the tall Lombardy poplars surrounding the house.

What celebrations there were that August day. Annie's head was spinning from the number of aunts, uncles, cousins and neighbours she was introduced to. When the dancing finally got under way she was in great demand and danced with everyone from Grandpa down to the twins. She was drinking a well-deserved glass of cool lemonade from the fast-emptying barrel when suddenly Carl materialised beside her. He looked at her appraisingly. Her long curly hair was even curlier than usual with the exertion of the dance and her cheeks were flushed. He had not realised how very pretty she was until now.

'You haven't danced with me yet, Annie,' he said, smiling at her.

'Well you haven't asked me,' she replied. He said nothing but replaced her empty glass beside the barrel, took her hand and led her back into the barn.

By now she had picked up the intricacies of the square dance and they joined the next set. What fun it was to dance, especially with someone as expert as Carl. He was tall and handsome too, she noticed for the first time. Not blond like Eric but dark like his father. On and on they went until she begged for mercy and they collapsed laughing on a bench outside.

'You had better get yourself another partner,' gasped Annie. 'I'm done.'

'I don't want another partner,' Carl replied, suddenly serious, looking down at her. 'I'm happy to be with you.'

Annie felt suddenly shy, not knowing quite how to respond to his sudden interest. She had already seen how popular Carl was among the girls and she was sure he had his choice of sweethearts.

Just then there was a call for everyone to assemble to bid farewell to the bridal couple, who were about to depart on their wedding journey north-east to Chicago. They were already installed in a barouche which would take them to the railway station in Omaha.

'Goodbye, goodbye,' called the assembled guests. Standing up in the open carriage, Gertrude, now dressed sensibly for the journey, threw her wedding bouquet over her shoulder. All the females, young and old, scrambled for it but it landed right in Annie's outstretched arms. Everyone laughed heartily as she blushed with embarrassment and buried her face in the scented bundle as the children gathered round shouting, 'You're the next bride, Annie.'

Catching Carl's eyes on her, Annie felt more embarrassed than ever and hurried into the house with the other girls.

12

DANGER ON THE PRAIRIE

On the day after the wedding, before she returned to Lincoln, Annie explained to Gertrude's Aunt Marthe her interest in training to be a teacher. It turned out that not only was Aunt Marthe a schoolteacher herself but she knew many of the staff of the Teachers' Institute in Lincoln. A tall, dignified, white-haired lady, Annie had at first found her a little intimidating but had soon warmed to her straightforward, no-nonsense attitude and sound advice.

'It is already in your favour that you have experience,' she had told Annie. 'I am sure you would be considered a good candidate for a training course. The fact that you have not finished public school might come against you but then, from what you say, the standard of education you had achieved before you came to America was very good. I will be very happy to arrange an interview for you. And as I am not due back at school myself for another couple of weeks, I will also be happy to show you around our city.'

Annie had been grateful for her kindness and advice

and it was agreed that the following week she would visit Lincoln, where she would stay with Aunt Marthe and explore what the institute had to offer.

Life in Miller's Creek had resumed its normal routine in the aftermath of the wedding. The house was remarkably quiet, with the men back working in the fields from morning till night. So Annie was surprised a couple of days later when Carl asked her to ride out on the prairie with him.

'I promised to look after Eric's herd down in the south-west quarter,' he explained. 'Besides I want to see if you can really manage a horse.'

Half-reluctant, Annie agreed to go, unable to resist the challenge. She had been a little uncomfortable with Carl since the night of the wedding and although she had been flattered by his attentions, she had avoided being alone with him since. Although she didn't quite understand why, something had changed between them. Until she had danced with him in the barn on the night of the wedding, Carl had treated her much as he would his sisters, whereas now – well, it was just not quite the same and she didn't know how she felt about that.

Carl had the horses saddled and ready to go shortly after breakfast and, taking a packed lunch from the kitchen, they rode out together, leaving word that they would be back in time for supper.

Annie need not have had any worries. Carl was his usual cheerful self and an excellent companion, pointing out everything of interest in the landscape. They spent some time watching the antics of prairie dogs –

comical little animals – through Carl's telescope. Annie didn't find it so comical though when Carl told her how snakes hibernated in the prairie dogs' burrows for the winter.

They picnicked on a rocky outcrop which gave them a wonderful view of the countryside. Later Annie helped Carl round up Eric's cattle and earned his praise for her skills on horseback.

'You've learned fast,' he said simply, but his look of warm admiration made Annie pleased she'd come.

As they turned to take the long trail home Carl kept glancing back westwards. Finally he stopped and took out his telescope and after looking intently for a minute or two said, 'I don't like the look of that sky, Annie. Somethin's brewin' and I hope it's just a storm.'

'Why, Carl, what else could it be? Besides, we can shelter at those rocks until it blows over can't we?' They weren't too far from the rocky outcrop they'd picnicked at earlier in the day.

Carl didn't reply and with a terse, 'Let's get going,' he set off at a gallop. Annie followed him but she was puzzled. What a pace he had set. Maybe he was just putting her to the test. He kept glancing back to see that she was keeping up so she had no real fear that she would get left behind. Anyway, Star, the strong young horse he'd chosen for her – belonging to Gertrude – was a joy to ride so she found the gallop exhilarating – this was the fastest she'd ever ridden.

After a while, however, seeing Carl constantly glancing over his shoulder, she became uneasy and, glancing back herself, suddenly became frightened. There was something about this oncoming storm that was very strange. What looked like a huge dark cloud seemed to be rolling fast towards them.

'We're heading for those rocks, Annie,' Carl shouted back at her. He had slowed his pace until she was almost level with him, near enough for her to see that he was quite agitated. She urged Star on. I must not panic, she thought to herself. Carl knows what to do. They drew up at the rocks. Carl came swiftly to help her dismount. Breathless, he placed his two hands on her shoulders and looked down at her sternly.

'Annie, this is no storm; it's a prairie fire and it's comin' this way. Now you have to do exactly what I tell you. Try not to be frightened. I know what I'm doing. It's comin' so fast we can't make it home from here so we're going to have to make a back fire to keep safe. We're lucky to have these rocks – they'll help to protect us. Now we must act fast, do you hear me, Annie, fast!'

Annie could hardly believe her ears. A prairie fire! Remembering the horrifying tales John had told them about prairie fires on Christmas night, she froze with fear. Pray God it wasn't true. She could die right here, out on the prairie without anyone knowing what had happened to her!

'Annie, for land sakes move! There's not a second to be wasted. Help me tie up the horses!'

The urgency of Carl's voice shocked Annie into action. It was no easy task now to secure the animals, who were showing signs of extreme nervousness and couldn't hold still, whinnying and trying to pull away. But with her help Carl managed to tie them to a small scrub tree protruding from the fissure between the rocks.

'You stay with them Annie – it's the best thing you can do. Try and calm them.' As he spoke Carl pulled his shirt over his head and tore it into two strips and, giving her one half, he began to tie the other around his horse's eyes. 'So as they won't see the fire. It would make them crazy,' he gasped. Annie imitated him, doing the same thing with Star. That done, she clung to the horses, her head thrust between them, trying her best to talk softly and calmly to them. But they could feel her fear and continued to shift restlessly, chafing against the rope and tossing their heads.

Meanwhile, Carl had started to burn the grass surrounding the rock mass in order to create a barren circle that the advancing fire couldn't feed on. He only had matches to complete the job – he'd never do it before the fire was upon them. Annie was rigid with terror. She could now see what was a wall of fire at least twelve feet high accompanied by huge clouds of billowing smoke advancing relentlessly towards them, covering the entire plain they had just raced across. It was a terrifying sight.

But the short scrub grass took fire and burned off quickly, leaving a blackened patch which was becoming wider and wider the harder Carl worked. Not a minute too soon. The towering wall of flame was getting nearer and nearer and Annie could now hear an overwhelming roaring noise as it approached. They were trapped now. The backfire would work or they would perish. Dear Lord, she prayed, spare us, please spare us.

She was pressed flat against the rock now, clinging for dear life to the two frantic animals, who at this stage were screaming and plunging in panic. She'd never have held them if they hadn't been tied. Carl, having done all he could was now with them and all four, humans and animals, cow,ered together to await their fate. First came billows of acrid-smelling smoke, whirling all around them, making them cough and splutter and then, encircling them, a world of flames stood, threatening to engulf them!

Miraculously the back fire worked and the circle of barren ground all around them held the flames back, protecting them from this vicious and overpowering enemy. Then suddenly it was over. The air cleared: the fire had passed right over them and rolled onwards, leaving them totally unscathed. Great sobs shook Annie and, holding her close, Carl soothed her.

'It's over, Annie. It's over. Look. Open your eyes. It's gone. We're going to be just fine.'

'It's just that I . . . ' Annie spluttered, unable to stem the tears of relief from pouring down her face. 'It's just that I nearly died in a fire once and I thought . . . '

Smoothing her hair back, Carl looked down at her tear-stained face, all blackened from the smoke, and saw how truly terrified she had been. Gently he bent down and kissed her very tenderly. 'Didn't you know I could take care of you?' he asked, smiling at her.

'You saved my life, Carl,' she replied, laying her head wearily on his chest.

After a few minutes, they moved to untie the poor horses, who were still trembling nervously. They removed the tattered remains of Carl's shirt from their eyes and patted them down, speaking soft, comforting words. Somewhat recovered now, although still shaking from her ordeal, Annie looked around, astonished at the blackened plains stretching out on all sides, dotted with patches which were still smoking.

Carl was as good as his word, and opening his saddlebag, he took out some bread, some fruit and a flagon of water, put Annie sitting down on the rocks and made her partake of most of it. She began to feel better.

This was not the first time he had endured such an experience, he explained to Annie. 'We used to get prairie fires more often when I was a kid. They're rare now. I don't know why. We sure were lucky to have got to this place in time, though. It would have been a lot more risky trying to set a backfire out in the open without any rocks. And even more frightening,' he added.

Annie looked at him in amazement. There he sat, cool as a breeze, looking as if this was almost an everyday occurrence. And he had just saved their lives!

'But let's get back. They'll be worried. Pa and the boys will probably have set off to look for us.'

Before long, they were on their way back, riding slowly and carefully over the scarred and smoky plains. Darkness was drawing in as they neared Miller's Creek and right enough they were met by a posse of family and neighbours riding out to meet them, armed with lanterns. There were relieved shouts of, 'Carl, Annie, is that you?' and 'Thank God!' as they drew near.

A great fuss was made of Annie that night. The

womenfolk helped her bathe and dress in clean clothes before sitting her before the stove and plying her with warm broth, Johanna scolding Carl for having got Annie into such a scrape in the first place.

'That was much too far to take the girl, Carl. And then to think that she was caught in a prairie fire! God's sake, Carl, what were you thinking of ?'

Later in bed Annie fell into an exhausted sleep and dreamt the whole terrifying episode through again – with one strange variation. It was Mike – not Carl – who had kissed her.

While Annie suffered not even a scrape from her adventure, she was nonetheless quite upset by the experience and for the first time since she had left New York she began to suffer from homesickness. She suddenly longed to see her family again – it was nearly a year since she'd left. She could not but remember her father's warnings about the hazards of life out in the West and how little she had heeded him. The Lindgren family were very kind to her and Carl was especially attentive, but she couldn't help feeling relieved that she would be leaving for Lincoln within a few days.

She was confused about Carl and when she was alone she tried to sort out what exactly she felt towards him. While she found him very attractive and had liked it when he kissed her, she felt she didn't really know him at all. Look what had happened when she thought she had known Robert Van der Leuten. But this was different – she could see quite clearly that Carl was falling in love with her. Perhaps she was in love too but she didn't realise it. Was this what love was, she wondered. It was just as well she was going off to Lincoln. It would be easier to sort it all out when she was away from him.

*

The morning of departure came and it was time, yet again, to bid her goodbyes to the family. They had been kindness itself and she was under strict orders from Gertrude's mama to come and stay as often as she possibly could, should she decide to stay on in Lincoln.

Again Carl drove her to the railway station at Omaha. Annie had recovered her spirits and they talked and laughed in their usual lively manner. However, when they drew up at the station, Carl, looking suddenly serious, took her hand in his and looked at her.

'Annie, you don't know how much I'll miss you,' he began, very hesitantly, for it wasn't really in Carl's nature to make serious speeches.

'Why, Carl, I will miss you too but we will see each other often, I'm sure, if I stay on in Lincoln to study,' replied Annie reassuringly, but inwardly she felt suddenly shy with him again.

'I know, Annie, but . . . ' Here he hesitated again. 'Darn it, Annie, I'm in love with you. You know that,' he exploded, looking away from her suddenly.

Somehow, Annie had known what he was going to say and she could see how much it cost him to say it, but for some reason she hadn't wanted him to say it. Not yet. It was too soon. She couldn't be sure she could say it back to him yet.

'Carl,' she began, 'Carl, I am not sure how I feel yet. I like you very much,' she added quickly, seeing him look anxiously at her. 'But I don't even know yet if I will stay on in Lincoln or if I shall return to New York or, for that matter, go back to Kimball.'

But now that Carl had told her how he felt, he seemed relieved and took her reaction well. 'Well, maybe you'll know more about it when you come back to stay,' he said, looking more cheerful. 'You promised to come back, mind,' he added. Then he jumped from the trap and swung her down and hugged her hard before releasing her. Blushing, Annie was glad to have to bend to retrieve her hat, which had fallen off in such a quick descent. But Carl, not even noticing, tied up the horses, grabbed the luggage and busied himself in getting her on to the Lincoln train.

13

A HAPPY REUNION

Within a few days of arriving in Lincoln, Annie knew she would jump at the chance to stay there rather than return to Kimball. It was almost like being back in New York. The capital city of Nebraska was a large, flourishing centre, both more handsome and more sophisticated than its sister city Omaha. It boasted a fine university and many splendid buildings, especially the opera house, which Aunt Marthe informed Annie was the finest Romanesque building west of Chicago. While Annie was impressed by this, what she liked best was the sight of so many young people of her own age in and around the university. It seemed almost everyone was a student. And even better, Aunt Marthe told her, there was a wonderful social life which welcomed people of all ages and backgrounds to discussion clubs and literary and political societies. Annie was agog with excitement at the thought of leading such a life.

'Now, if you are accepted at the institute you won't have too much free time,' Aunt Marthe reminded her. 'Don't forget, you'll have to work during the day to complete teaching practice and then I'd reckon most evenings will be spent at classes and studying your books.' Aunt Marthe was a realist and Annie came down to earth with a bang.

It was just as well they were realistic as it was not all as smooth sailing as Annie had hoped. While an interview was relatively simple to arrange, the outcome was not. In normal circumstances, Miss Howard, the principal, explained, Annie would be expected to have graduated from public school before being accepted. However, due to the shortage of teachers in Nebraska as well as her short stint as an assistant teacher in Kimball she would be granted an exemption but – and Annie quailed in her boots when she heard the 'but' – she would be obliged to pass an entrance examination before being accepted for this year's course.

'Of course you will succeed, we'll see to that,' Aunt Marthe said briskly as they left the solid brick building together in the afternoon sunshine.

'But I only have two weeks,' Annie said doubtfully.

Aunt Marthe was as good as her word. She wasted not a moment and organised Annie's study schedule like a general organising a military campaign. The first thing Annie must do, she said, was to write to Miss Hammond in Kimball and relinquish her position at the school. She could do so this very evening. Before Annie had time to blink she found herself sitting at Aunt Marthe's fine walnut desk with pen, ink and notepaper. Aunt Marthe was an old-fashioned teacher – the type you obeyed instantly. When she had written to Miss Hammond of her intentions she decided not to waste any more time but to write home to her parents and Molly and Sophia as well as to Ellen and Dan, confiding her hopes and plans. Somehow, writing the letters confirmed her commitment and was, therefore, the biggest step of all. Once she had that task out of the way, she felt ready for the challenge ahead of her – as Aunt Marthe guessed she would.

'Now, we shall start with arithmetic – that will soon banish the cobwebs from our heads,' began Aunt Marthe the following morning as she settled Annie down at one side of her large desk while she sat at the other side. A large selection of books were already piled up on a side table.

She was a good teacher, Annie soon discovered, marvelling at her own good luck and apprehensive that Aunt Marthe might find her stupid. But she soon became engrossed and the morning passed in the blink of an eye. And so it went on. The days flew by, with Aunt Marthe spending each morning tutoring Annie and leaving her to absorb what she had learned each afternoon.

All of a sudden it was the day of the examination and she found herself sitting in the college hall with a group of young people of around her own age. Annie closed her eyes and took a deep breath – Aunt Marthe's recipe for achieving a calm state – and told herself that she would try her very best but that even if she failed she could still go back to Kimball or perhaps even New York and find some work. After all, she had her new-found skill at stenography to fall back on.

The only sounds that broke the silence for the rest of that day were the scratching of nibs, the rustle of paper and the occasional deep sigh of despair or satisfaction as each and every student struggled to overcome the final hurdle that stood between them and their dreams.

Annie felt she had not acquitted herself as well as she would have liked, but later on, discussing it all with Aunt Marthe, she was encouraged to think she had not done so badly after all, and she nurtured the quiet hope over the next couple of days that she would be admitted to the institute.

'Now, all that remains is for you to find work in a school,' declared Aunt Marthe cheerfully the morning the good news arrived in a letter bearing the institute's insignia. She didn't seem in the least surprised. Annie was thrilled and read the letter over and over again. It was the first real examination she had ever sat and she had passed. How she wished her parents were here at this proud moment. She would have to write straightaway and tell them, but Aunt Marthe, practical as always, had broken into her reverie.

'Now, child, let us make plans. You will need to register in the college and then set about finding work in a school immediately. There's not a moment to be wasted.'

Aunt Marthe had already offered Annie lodging at a nominal rate, which she had gratefully accepted. Looking for a place to live would have been an extra worry and expense. Besides, Annie now realised that without Aunt Marthe's help and support she would most likely never have been able to progress this far.

'You have been very kind to me, Miss Lindgren, I

can't thank you enough,' she said warmly when, following the arrival of the letter, Aunt Marthe moved a small desk into the room Annie occupied on the first floor of the neat terraced house in the town.

'I like to see young people making their way in the world, especially when they are halfway there already through their own efforts,' Aunt Marthe replied, adding, 'and since you are going to live here for a while you may please call me Aunt Marthe.'

By the time term started, Annie had found a job as a trainee assistant teacher in a school quite near the college. Aunt Marthe, coming to her aid yet again, had supplied her with a letter of character. That, as well as the fact that she was a registered student at the Teachers' Institute, made finding a job an easy enough task. According to Aunt Marthe most of the schools were short-staffed and crying out for teachers, especially in Lincoln.

Marymount School was far better equipped than the small school at Kimball. It had fine, big classrooms and a plentiful supply of books. However, to Annie's disappointment, she was not put in charge of one particular group of children but had to move between classes as she was needed, either to take the place of a teacher who was absent or to help one who was over-burdened with work. Nonetheless, she enjoyed it and felt she had made the right choice.

Once school was through, she would rush home, have something to eat and do some preparation for her classes at the college, which started at six o'clock on three evenings a week.

Reaction to Annie's move to Lincoln arrived over the next couple of weeks in the form of a deluge of letters, from both New York and Scott's Bluff.

'I can't tell you how proud we are of you, Annie,' Mother wrote. 'To think of you a schoolteacher! Norah says to tell you that she had a letter from Cork with the news that Julia Donohue has also become a teacher but it's the music she teaches. We're longing to see you and hear all about your adventures so I hope it won't be long before you return to New York and maybe get a fine job here.' Even Father added in a few words of encouragement at the end of Mother's letter.

Molly too was quick to write and wish her well. Her letter was full of herself and Tom and their plans to become betrothed by Christmas. 'But it's a close secret, Annie, so don't breathe it to a soul yet,' she added.

If Annie had not been so very busy, all this rush of news from home would have made her very homesick indeed. She did reflect on it in bed at night and wondered how long it would be before she saw them all again. A year anyway until the course is finished and I get my certificate, she reflected. More and more though, she felt drawn back towards city life, and she thought she would probably return to New York eventually. Her thoughts then turned to Carl and she wondered what he would have to say to that. She wondered again if she was in love with him – it would be nice after all to be in love with someone who was in love with you, but when she thought about stories she had read and the real life people she had seen, she knew that this was not the way love was at all. Yet she was very fond of him.

Of Mike there was no word from any quarter. Again she comforted herself with the thought that if he was betrothed by now, someone would have mentioned it – if not Molly then her parents or Tom.

There was also news from Scott's Bluff. Ellen had written, full of enthusiasm for Annie's plans – 'We knew you'd make good in Lincoln' – but had her own news to announce too: 'The house is all but finished. We should be installed in it by next month and just in time, as I'm with child again and Scott is to have a baby brother or sister by next March.'

The weeks passed quickly as Annie became accustomed to the routine of teaching and study. Despite having very little free time, she managed to enjoy herself and had joined the Students' Political Society.

Early one evening as she was on her way home from a lecture at the institute she noticed that there was a great air of excitement around the railway station. Crowds of people were gathered, many of them holding banners aloft. Some political meeting, Annie thought to herself and, stooping, picked up a handbill which had fallen to the ground.

NATIONAL POLITICIAN AND EDITOR OF THE OMAHA WORLD HERALD, WILLIAM JENNINGS BRYAN, WILL ADDRESS A POPULIST PARTY RALLY AT LINCOLN OPERA HOUSE ON 17 OCTOBER 1895. ALL WELCOME!

Of course, Annie recalled, this was the politician all
Nebraska was talking about . . . the one she'd heard tell
of from Scott's Bluff to Miller's Creek. A Democrat and
a big shot in Washington but also the darling of
Nebraska's farmers.

'What's happening?' Annie asked a woman bearing
a banner with **JUSTICE FOR NEBRASKA FARMERS**
printed on it in bold black print.

'It's William Jennings Bryan, he's due to arrive any
minute now from Omaha for the rally at the opera
house tonight,' the woman replied excitedly.

'He's our only hope,' declared a ruddy-faced farmer,
who held a similar banner.

There was a further stir of excitement as they heard
the announcement of the train's arrival on the loud
hailer. Overcome by curiosity to see the great man in
person, Annie stood with the crowd. They hadn't long
to wait until a large party appeared at the main entrance to the station and then the cheering started as
the people's hero emerged and, breaking free from his
escorts, stepped forward to address the crowd. Annie
noted that he was a fine-looking, powerfully built man
with thick dark hair.

'Good people of Lincoln, I'm happy to be returning
home today to speak with you,' he began in a great
booming voice. 'I bring with me some visitors from the
great Democratic Party in the East. They want to be sure
that I don't stray too far from the party line. But party
or no party, I'm here to listen to your problems – and
to make sure that they hear them too and at last
understand what the past few years have been like for

the farmers of Nebraska,' he finished, his voice rising passionately. At this there was wild cheering from the delighted crowd.

Suddenly Annie saw him. Standing slightly apart from the party accompanying the famous man was a familiar figure. Tall and every bit as handsome as the former congressman was someone who made her heart beat so fast she all but fainted. Mike! What was he doing here in Nebraska. Could it really be him?

Struggling through the crowd towards the steps, Annie was conscious of no one but Mike. She simply must speak with him. If he disappeared now she might not get another opportunity.

The great man, having concluded his short speech, was about to move to the waiting line of horse-cabs which would bear him and his entourage to the opera house. They began to descend the steps. And then Mike saw Annie. His face lit up and, hastening towards each other, they all but collided.

'Annie!'

'Mike! What are you doing here?'

Laughing incredulously, they hugged until Mike, holding her at arm's length, looked at her admiringly.

'The West certainly suits you, Annie.'

'Whatever are you doing here in Lincoln, Mike?' Annie repeated, still astounded at the sight of him.

Mike laughed, retorting, 'I could well ask you the same question only I already know the answer because Molly has been keeping me posted. But to answer your question, you could say I'm here for the rally as a political observer from Tammany Hall but I'm also here to see a friend of mine from New York and ask her why she never writes me any letters.'

Embarrassed, Annie looked up at him shyly and saw that although he was smiling, the question had a serious edge to it. She was lost for words, so full was she of confused thoughts – remembering how angry and heartbroken she had been when she had parted from him in New York a year previously, her conviction that he must love Clara, the impressions she had received from Molly and finally, the knowledge of how much she had missed him. And now here he was, suddenly, asking why she hadn't written to him. She no longer knew what to think.

'Molly gave me your address so I could find you. But here you are,' he declared with delight.

'It's quite a coincidence.' Annie had found her voice at last. 'I was on my way home from a lecture and I saw the crowd and joined them to see what was happening ... and then ... well I just couldn't believe it when I saw you. How long will you stay?'

'Just a couple of days. Remember I am still a humble tailor in New York. Will you come with me to the rally? Now that I've found you I don't want to lose sight of you. You might just disappear again.'

How could Annie refuse. Within minutes she found herself being borne away in a horse cab to the opera house with Mike, part of the lively party surrounding the great Lincoln politician. Swept up in the excitement of the rally, there was little time to speak with each other again until it was over. Annie sat quietly and watched while Mike took notes and consulted with other members of the party.

Occasionally, he flashed her a quick smile as if to say 'I haven't forgotten you're here', and finally, it was all over and he was escorting her home. As they walked along together they were silent at first until Mike said, 'I know you must be surprised to see me and perhaps I should have written and let you know but I was afraid if I did that you might not agree to meet me.'

Agree to meet him? Annie looked at him sharply to see if he was serious. But it appeared he was.

'I would never have refused to see you, Mike,' she said simply.

'Perhaps then we can meet tomorrow and have a long talk because we have much to talk about,' replied Mike.

It was too late to bring him in to meet Aunt Marthe so the young couple lingered at the door talking. Eventually it was arranged that Mike should meet Annie outside the school the following day after she had finished work.

Annie hardly slept a wink. She hardly knew whether it was happiness at seeing Mike or dread that he should yet tell her that he was betrothed to someone else. Clara had not been mentioned but perhaps that was what he meant when he said they had much to talk about. And what part had Molly played in all of this she wondered. She had never mentioned anything about Mike in any of her letters. Yet she couldn't escape the impression that he had been delighted to see her and had hugged her with every bit as much warmth as she had hugged him. How would she wait until tomorrow when she would see him again. She would have to tell Aunt Marthe about him – perhaps bring him back to meet her. But no, she wanted to spend some time with him first. How could they talk with Aunt Marthe there too?

Eventually she fell asleep, none the wiser but inexplicably happier than she had been for some time.

Next morning she was up earlier than usual and took extra-special care with her dress. Over breakfast, she told Aunt Marthe about Mike and promised to bring him to meet her later on.

'Take care you do that then, Annie. I was plenty worried about you last evening,' replied Aunt Marthe, looking a little put out. 'I didn't know where you had got to. I trust this young man is known to your parents?'

'Oh yes, Aunt Marthe, he's a very old friend of all my family. He's been almost like a brother to me.'

Aunt Marthe glanced sceptically at her young lodger over her spectacles, noting the extra special effort she had put into her appearance, but she said nothing. She was no fool and Annie certainly did not have the demeanour of someone whose brother had come to visit.

Annie's heart leapt when she saw Mike pacing up and down outside the school when classes finally ended that afternoon. She could still hardly believe he was really here.

At first they were both a little awkward with one another but as they walked along they relaxed and began to talk. Firstly, Mike told her all about his job and of course, his political work. He was doing very well as a tailor and his original plan to open his own business was looking more realistic every day. His interest in politics was as lively as ever and as she could see for herself, he was now a trusted and active member of the Democratic Party. Annie enjoyed hearing all about his life and wondered if she should ask about Clara, but before she could do so Mike said, 'But tell me what you've been doing Annie. I have heard some of it from Molly and Tom – it sounds as if you have had great adventures.'

It was a golden autumn day. They sat down on a bench under the shade of a chestnut tree, its remaining leaves turned to russet. Annie told him all about her months out on the prairies of west Nebraska living in the sod-house with Ellen and Dan, about the rough conditions of life there as well as the beauty of the landscape, about baby Scott's dramatic arrival and finally about her job in Kimball, where she had made the discovery that she wanted to become a teacher.

When she came to the end of her account, Mike was looking at her in open admiration. He saw someone who, in a year, had matured into a beautiful and independent young woman. He had always thought her attractive, with her good looks and lively personality, but there was a beauty and grace about her now born of her experiences in the past year that made him look at her with new eyes.

'How you've changed, Annie. You have seen more of America now than many people and had such grand experiences,' he said. He sighed and looked up at the canopy of leaves immediately above them. 'Do you think of returning to New York,' he asked abruptly.

'Of course I do, Mike, and I intend to but I want to finish the course at the institute first.' She saw he was looking at her closely and listening intently so she continued.

'You see, Mike, I don't want to return to New York until I make something of myself. I felt trapped there. I don't wish to go back into service. I made good money at it but learned nothing and had no freedom to do anything. Thanks to Molly's advice I managed to get some lessons in stenography and typewriting, which gave me some possibility of working as an office clerk but I would need more training. I really came out west to discover what I wanted to do with myself and to get away from New York. I've seen so much in the past year. It's a completely different life out here – a harder life in some ways but a good life. I thought for a while that I should never want to return to New York but I guess I miss my folks a lot and if I could get work as a teacher I would be happy to try it out again. But I must get my certificate first.'

'I could help you get work, Annie. I still do some teaching at the night school and I know lots of teachers.' He paused for a moment. 'Annie ... you know, I would really like you to come back. I've missed you. I only realised how much after you left New York. I know we had hardly seen one another since you went into service. And then ... ' He stopped suddenly and looked at her.

Her heart in her mouth, Annie said, 'But what

about Clara? Are you and she . . . ?' She couldn't bring herself to ask.

Mike looked at her and, taking her hand in both of his, he looked down at it for a moment.

'Clara is a fine girl. We walked out for a while together last year but . . . well I soon discovered that we had little in common. She wanted me to become someone different to what I was. We are still friends but there is no understanding between us.

'You remember when me met last, Annie? You were angry with me and with very good reason. I should not have tried to hold you back. I didn't want to but your parents persuaded me to try and influence you and I felt I had to . . . well, perhaps deep down I didn't want you to go either. But when you became angry with me, I suddenly saw it all from your point of view. It changed everything. I wanted to say that but you were so angry and then you left. I stayed there for a long time thinking about you that night and I think it was then that I realised I was beginning to fall in love with you. But I knew I had to let you go. And then finally, a few weeks ago, when I knew I would get the chance to come out here to the rally, I decided to confide in Molly. I made her promise not to say anything to you in her letters. I was afraid if she did . . . '

'You need not have been afraid, Mike,' said Annie very softly.

Mike, seeing her expression, took her in his arms. He leaned down and kissed her as he had been longing to do since the moment he had set eyes on her at the station.

'I love you, Annie Moore. I think I've loved you since the day I first saw you on the tender at Queenstown.'